THIEF'S BODYGUARD

HUNT SECURITY, BOOK 1

JASMINE C. CALDWELL

Contents

He showed up for this gig expecting a spoiled society girl.
Instead, he found his feisty fling.

Jenna's starting over. She's got a new name, a new town, and a new job—one that's legal this time. Her criminal days are over. To keep herself safe, she needs to lie low. Ahot hookup gives her memories that she can't erase. Then her estranged father hires the guy—as her bodyguard! When he shows up at her door, her cover's blown.

Roger never sees the same woman more than once. He can't afford the distraction—been there, done that. Keeping his security business afloat is the top priority, and he just got the offer of a lifetime. Until he discovers that his new charge is the one-night stand that haunts his dreams. And she's pissed about it.

How is Roger supposed to protect someone who fights him at every turn? And what will he say when Jenna's secrets are exposed?

Dear Mom and Dad,
If you read this, you were warned.
Love,
Your Daughter

Chapter 1

THE BUS DROVE AWAY from the corner where Jenna O'Malley stood, sharp eyes sweeping the neighborhood for danger. She shifted her duffel bag higher on her shoulder and marked the numbers of the row-houses as she kicked an empty beer can out of her way. It bounced over the weeds bursting through jagged cracks in the sidewalk.

This area of Baltimore had seen better days, that was for sure, but the red brick buildings looked sturdy enough. And it would be harder to pinpoint her location when they were all similar. But she didn't expect her former bosses to sniff out her trail. She'd gotten across the country in record time. They probably hadn't even missed her yet.

She strolled for a couple of blocks in the summer sun until she came to number fourteen and a half. Avoiding the rusty railing, she descended the six stairs to the basement unit and knocked. Almost immediately, the white door with peeling paint opened to reveal a bubbly blonde-haired girl with bright blue eyes.

"Hi! I'm Erin. You must be Amber! Come on in!"

"Thanks," Jenna replied, responding to the fake name she'd given over the phone. Erin was younger than her, still in her twenties, it seemed. She wore a hoodie that made Jenna's stomach clench.

"Baltimore Police Department? You work there?"

Maybe it was her boyfriend's shirt? That sounded like an even worse prospect. Jenna didn't want anyone associated with the cops anywhere near her.

"Hmm? Well, technically. I'm a dispatcher."

She breathed a sigh of relief when Erin turned around. A dispatcher she could handle.

"Let me give you a tour."

The basement apartment was bigger on the inside than she had thought at first glance. She followed Erin around the living area that was just big enough for a two-seater couch and a television. A breakfast bar with three stools divided the kitchen from the living room.

"We even have a dishwasher, which is *such* a godsend after a graveyard shift."

The appliances weren't brand new, but they seemed in decent shape, and the shared bathroom was small but mold-free.

At the back of the building, a twin-size bed and a dresser stood along the far wall of a small but clean bedroom. "My old roommate just got engaged and moved in with her fiancé. She said she doesn't need the furniture. It's yours if you want it. I washed the sheets with the rest of my laundry last week, so no one's slept in them."

Jenna stopped and looked at her. "You're going to rent it to me?"

Erin leaned against the wall out in the hallway where she stood. "Listen, I can't go another month without a roommate, and you're the most normal one that's responded to my ad. The last girl wouldn't shut up about her toenail clippings collection." Erin shuddered and made a gagging noise. Jenna just raised her brows. She could pretend to be normal. Fake it until you make it, right?

"Anyway, we split utilities and groceries down the middle, but if there's anything special you don't want to share, keep it in your room. I put my shifts on the calendar in the kitchen, and I'd like you to do the same. I expect shared spaces to get cleaned if you make a mess. We switch off every other week for chores, except garbage. Garbage night is Tuesday, and that goes to whoever doesn't have to work."

Jenna nodded. This all seemed totally reasonable.

"I don't care what you do in your bedroom as long as there are no bug infestations, and I get my sleep." Erin knocked on the wall behind her. "They're not very thick. Just please wear headphones if you're gonna watch porn or have phone sex with your partner."

At that idea, Jenna snorted. "No partner, no problem."

Erin shrugged. "You're pretty. It could happen."

Not a chance. Jenna's old life hadn't allowed for attachments. Despite all she'd changed and left behind, the danger that came with deep human connection remained.

Her new roommate cocked her head. "Do you have a job yet?"

Jenna nodded. "Just got a job waiting tables at Urban Roadhouse." They'd been desperate, and so had she. When she walked in and asked about the help wanted sign in the window, the manager had hired her on sight. He'd wanted her to start tonight, but she explained she was moving and had to see an apartment. Erin was the only one who knew she was new to town. The less other people knew about her, the better.

She slid her bag off her shoulder onto the floor and kneeled to dig into the outside pocket where she'd put her rent money. "I can give you the first month's rent in cash, if that works."

"Sure. I already paid for the utilities this month. I'll give you a break on that."

"About how much do they run?"

Erin named a number, and Jenna added half that amount to the wad of cash she handed her.

"Are you sure?"

Jenna nodded and rose to her feet. "I don't want to stiff you."

Erin quickly shuffled through the cash and stuck it into her pocket. Jenna respected that she didn't trust her blindly. You could never be too careful. "Well, I won't argue. When can you move in?"

She gestured to the black bag sitting on the floor. "This is all I could take with me."

"Oh, my gosh!" Erin gasped and her eyes about popped out of her head. She gulped. "Did he — did he *hurt* you?"

When she'd called the number on the "Roommate Wanted" flyer in the bar, Jenna had insinuated that she was on the run from an abusive uncle. Continuing the lie, she shook her head. "I didn't give him the chance. I saw my opening, and I took it."

Erin breathed a sigh of relief. "I'm so glad. You poor thing. How about I order a pizza while you get unpacked? My treat."

Oh, you sweet, innocent thing. You have no idea who I'm really running from.

"Pizza sounds great. Thanks, Erin." She might be smart, but she was definitely a touch gullible.

Which was exactly what Jenna needed her to be.

Unpacking took her all of five minutes, but Jenna took the opportunity to jump in the shower and wash off the grime of traveling. She'd ditched the last car she'd hot-wired a while back and had to finish her journey on the Greyhound. Mass transit wasn't her favorite, but it could have been worse. Hitchhiking would have made her really sweaty and gross.

After her shower, she swiped at the mirror over the sink. This new hair would take some getting used to. Her first stop on the run had been to a salon on her way out of Nevada. Their colorist had done a masterful job at hiding her natural copper hair, although the poor girl had nearly cried at the injustice. Nothing Jenna could do about it. Red hair stood out too much. The black dye was much better for blending in. Then she'd had them chop it off, right above her shoulders, and cover her forehead with bangs. Even her own mother wouldn't recognize her on the street, now.

Before she left the bathroom, Jenna covered her natural eyebrows in thick coats of black mascara. The small-town salon back in Texas hadn't had the equipment to dye them for her, but in a city like Baltimore, that shouldn't be a problem.

Erin called out just as she finished pulling on her pajamas. "Amber, pizza's here!"

She couldn't remember the last time she'd had a sleepover. College, maybe? Before her life went to hell.

Satisfied her appearance wouldn't give her away, Jenna strolled out to the hallway.

"Can you grab the extra napkins? They're in the hall closet!"

"Sure!"

When Jenna pulled the door open, a pile of weird foam implements assailed her, smacking into her braless breasts. "Ow!" Distracted, she bent over to pick one of them up. "What the hell?"

"Oh my God, I'm sorry! I must have been in too much of a rush last time." A blushing Erin stood before her and the pile of foam... weapons?

"It's fine."

Erin helped her pick up the harmless fake weapons and put them back into the closet. Then she grabbed the napkins from the top shelf, spying what looked like faux leather armor hanging on the rod inside.

What the fuck was her new roommate *into*?

"Come on, I'll explain over dinner."

Jenna followed Erin back to the main room, where a pizza box called from the breakfast bar with its enticing scent.

"That's where I keep my LARP weapons. I didn't have a lot of time after the last practice to get a shower and go to work. I must have been a bit sloppy putting them away."

Jenna discretely rubbed her sore boob and wondered if her roommate was speaking English. "What's LARP?"

Swallowing her bite of pizza, Erin continued. "It stands for Live Action Role Play." Her cheeks flushed red. "We're like, the nerds of the nerd world. Although the SCA might be worse than us... Anyway, the main concept is we fight in teams called nation-states, but the weapons won't really hurt you, as you can see."

"You just get together and beat each other with foam swords?"

"Or axes or arrows with soft pillows on the end. Anything you can justify as part of your culture, the judges will allow."

"Culture?"

Erin grinned with pride. "I am a member of the only all-female nation-state. It's called Themyscira."

Jenna cocked her head. "Like the mythical Greek island of the Amazons?"

"That's the one!" Erin reached for another slice of pepperoni. "We actually have an event coming up next week if you want to check it out."

"I don't know... I start at the Roadhouse tomorrow."

"It's in the middle of the week, just a one-night event. And I know most of the team won't be able to be there, so we'll need all the help we can get." Her tone turned cajoling. "There's always a party afterward."

Jenna sighed. Now that she'd left her old life behind, she found herself at loose ends. Who was this new person, this Amber Smith? This new identity was a blank slate that she could write however she wanted. While staring out the window of her bus as the highway blurred by, Jenna had promised to keep an open mind as far as her future went. As long as it had nothing to do with the specter of her past, she'd try anything once.

Plus, she wanted to get in her roommate's good graces, now that she knew she worked in law enforcement. Jenna needed Erin to trust her. And the game did sound intriguing. God knew her father wouldn't ever think to look for his precious daughter camping in the mud. And the company she used to keep wouldn't get their hands dirty, either.

That had been *her* job.

"And honestly? Pretty much anything goes at these things. These guys get *horny*."

How long had it been since Jenna had any fun of the carnal variety? Ages. Ever since she decided to get as far away as possible from Nevada, she hadn't even picked up a stranger in a bar. It had taken a long time to track down someone who could give her a convincing new identity, and even longer to extricate herself from her old life.

But Erin didn't seem the type.

"You strike me as a relationship girl. I would have thought you'd have a boyfriend."

Erin shrugged, her blonde curls bouncing off her shoulder. "I used to be. But there aren't a lot of guys who can put up with my work schedule. And if they *do* understand, it's because they've also got the schedule from hell, and we never see each other."

Jenna nodded in solidarity. "I can't do attachments, either."

"Why not?"

She couldn't tell Erin the real reason. "It's personal."

Her new roommate just shrugged it off. "So... Wanna go camping, beat up boys, and get laid next week?"

Chapter 2

Rain hung heavily in the early morning air as Roger Hunt sipped sparingly at his shitty instant coffee. Hopefully, the weather would hold until after their skirmish, or else this field would turn into a mud pit. But then, he wouldn't mind watching the female fighters wrestle in the mud. Seeing that would be worth delaying his post-battle shower.

"Arlas, hail!" Regen called out from their tent. His short, stout teammate raised the banner for Melberth in the center of their circle of tents, but not close enough to catch in the campfire. Gradually their team gathered in the center as players finished their preparations.

Regen's wife Jessica, or Jasmine as she was known in-game, was there as always. Along with Dax, their latest lover. He didn't bother to keep track. Roger had joked to his polyamorous friends once about a scorecard, and they'd responded by showing him the online calendar that linked all their relationships together. Being a one-night-stand man himself, his mind had boggled at the sight.

Roger didn't do relationships. As a member of the United States Special Forces, going on dangerous missions hadn't been compatible with romance. For half of his life, he'd avoided entanglements and attachments outside of his family. Then he retired a few years ago and started his security firm. And being the sole person working there, he still hadn't escaped the dangerous jobs. The stakes were generally lower, sure, but still present.

Or maybe, at forty-one, he was just set in his ways.

One of the judges approached their camp, her distinctive yellow tabard indicating her role in the game.

"Hail, Melberth! There has been a change in plan for today's battles." Roger and his teammates gathered around the LARP referee.

"What's changed?" Roger asked. While Cameron, known as Regen in-game, was technically in charge of their nation-state, Roger's character, Arlas, was their general.

"Due to the impending storms, we've decided to pair states up in battle and have you fight two-on-two."

A few grumbled. But the officials were making the right call as far as Roger was concerned. Camping in the rain wasn't too bad but beating each other with foam weapons would suck. Someone could get hurt. Better to get the fighting done as early as possible today.

"We've paired Melberth with Themiscyra against Sumer and Babylon. Your numbers will still be even. And your fight time has not changed. We will see you on the battle-field!"

Roger's brow furrowed. They'd never fought against Themiscyra, and he had no idea of their strategy. He often watched their battles, but he was usually too distracted by the all-female team who played as Amazons. Their armor showed a lot of skin.

He turned to Regen. "We should go over there and make a battle plan with Themiscyra."

"Agreed. Let's go, Arlas. We'll confer with their general."

Roger choked down the rest of his coffee and held up one finger. "Let me get my garb on first. I'll only be a minute." Regen nodded, and he ducked back into his bright blue tent. The coffee mug went back in with his other camping dishes and he hastily threw on his tabard and bracers, which showed his rank and nation's colors. He left his armor inside; he wouldn't need it until they were ready to fight. Exiting the tent, he quickly returned to Regen's side.

"Do you know where they're camped?" He asked, squinting at all the colorful banners in the area. This event wasn't as well attended as Armageddon, the big event every November. It was just a regional skirmish. Their Pennsylvanian rivals, Katan, weren't there, for instance, since they belonged to a different region. Even the teams were smaller. His siblings hadn't been able to make it out for various reasons. Jonathon was stuck in Annapolis during the week, Finn was stationed in Okinawa this year, and Nadia had to work. Her boyfriend Caleb did too, who was also a member of the nation. Many other teams were here with fewer people as well. Pairing up for battle should actually make things *more* interesting.

"The judge said their banner is red and blue." Regen was searching around as well. Roger had a foot on them height-wise, so he doubted they could see any more than he could.

"Is that it?" He pointed at a blue and red banner hanging in the distance.

"It's the only one I see, too. Let's go find out." Roger and Regen hiked through the camping ground. By his best estimate, it was a quarter mile across, and of course, Themiscyra had set up camp on the opposite side from them. But he wasn't worried. He had long legs and years of military experience marching through hellish conditions, wearing a dozen pounds of body armor, along with his weapons and other gear. This was just a minor annoyance.

He could tell right away they'd been correct. The camp was filled with women of all different flavors wearing their Amazonian armor. And it didn't leave much to the imagination. Part of him was delighted, and he looked forward to teasing his brothers about missing out. Jonathon was particularly familiar with the ladies of Themiscyra, though all the Hunt men had warmed various tents there over the years.

The other part of him, the tactician, was annoyed at the wrench thrown into the Melberth battle machine. But he pushed it down; the Amazons were not his enemy.

He followed Regen over to Hippolyta and General Antiope, women he was familiar with, but not in the biblical sense. They were more interested in each other.

The four met and spoke. A judge had also visited them with the news, and the Amazons were aware of the change. Roger fought to keep his focus on the conversation with their temporary allies, but his gaze kept flying behind Hippolyta to a pair of women sparring in the field.

"Erin, hang on!" one woman said to the other as she attacked.

"*Alete!*" The attacker, an athletic blonde, fisted her sword and put one hand on her hip.

"Sorry, Dydia. The name thing is weird." The defender shuffled from one foot to the other. Clearly, she was a new player. He couldn't see her face, since her back was facing him, but she had beautiful long black waves down to her shoulders. She was petite and slim, but she had curves in the right places.

The one called Dydia went over the combat rules again, Alete's dark hair blowing in the wind as she nodded along. Combat. He was supposed to be strategizing, and here he was ogling his allies. Fuck.

Returning his attention to the matter at hand, he managed to contribute to the conversation until all were satisfied they had a winning strategy. The topic changed to personal things as Regen socialized. Roger, however, was entranced by the raven-haired beauty in the field.

"I'm no good at this; I'm better at stealth," she complained to her friend.

"Yeah, you're a ninja at home. You're always scaring me when I don't think you're in the room."

Alete sighed. "I feel like this was a bad idea."

"Aw, come on. It'll be fun, I promise."

Roger had inched forward and watched them go at it again. Alete was too hesitant. She was clearly afraid to hurt her friend.

"Hail, ladies."

Dydia froze mid-strike, caught unaware, and Alete paused as well. Roger chuckled. "You know you just lost the perfect opportunity to strike her, right?"

Alete stammered, a blush rising to her pale, freckle-strewn cheeks. She was fucking gorgeous. And she definitely needed to spar with someone she didn't know. He looked over at Dydia. "Would you like some assistance?"

Dydia held out her hand. "Sure. I am Dydia. This is my friend, Alete, and it's her first battle."

Roger shook the blonde's hand politely. "I'm Arlas, of Melberth. We came over to discuss strategy with Hippolyta and Antiope."

"I'm looking forward to the battle. Melberth fights well," Dydia practically purred. Then he turned and held his hand out to Alete. When she put hers into his, he drew it to his lips and kissed her knuckles. Her piercing blue eyes widened, and her friend squeaked behind him.

"Why don't I spar with you, Alete? You don't have to be afraid of hurting a big berserker like me. I can take it."

Alete drew her hand back, but not before he clocked how fast the pulse in her wrist beat. Oh, yes, the little

Amazon was interested. And Roger wanted her in his tent tonight.

"Okay." Alete squared her shoulders and gripped her sword. "Let's see what you've got, big guy."

He showed her the same patience that he showed everyone he taught the game, carefully walking through moves and scenarios. That he made excuses to touch her as often as he could was beside the point. He had a little difficulty gauging her reactions; he couldn't look at her face while he adjusted her stance, and especially when he demonstrated how to swing her sword with his arms wrapped around her. At least her friend was not immune. He saw her eyebrows wag more than once at the beauty in his arms.

When it was unfortunately over, Alete turned to him, a rosy flush on her cheeks. "You're a good teacher."

Roger shrugged. "I've been doing this a long time."

"Arlas!" Regen called.

He had to go. "I'll see you on the battlefield, gorgeous." He gave her a wink and his sexiest grin as he returned to Regen to go back to their camp and update the other players on their new strategy.

"Where did you go, friend?" Regen smirked at him as they hiked back through the muddy campground.

"Themyscira has a new player, and she needed to spar with someone she wasn't afraid to hurt."

"Sure, that's all that was." His friend shook their head. "You're such a flirt, Arlas."

He grinned. "I've never actually had to pay attention to how the Amazons fought before. Usually we're spectators at their skirmishes."

"Doesn't hurt that she's pretty, hmm?"

"At least I won't be competing against my brothers this time. The younger ones usually go for Finn or Jon."

"Good luck with that. Not that you'll need it." Regen looked behind them, back at Themyscira's camp. "I didn't catch much, but I'm pretty sure she's interested."

Roger rubbed his hands together. He'd been having a bit of a dry spell lately; it was hard to find unattached women at his age on the bar scene, which meant he'd stopped going out at all. He had no interest in sleeping with someone half his age. Alete might be slightly younger, but she didn't strike him as naïve. Her demeanor had a worldly air that hinted at her maturity.

He couldn't wait for the battle now.

THIS PARTY HAD BETTER be the best one she'd ever been to if this was what she had to endure.

Jenna slid through the mud again, grateful she'd worn a pair of boots. Unfortunately, they were new and there was no way they'd survive this. But as long as *she* survived, she'd consider this a win.

Looking up, she gasped as an opposing player's sword swung down, but Arlas jumped to her defense. He beat them back easily. Under normal circumstances, Jenna would have been annoyed that he felt the need to come to her rescue, but she was completely out of her depth here.

Of course, as a muscular dude, this was totally his kind of game. The tall shield he carried helped, too. Why didn't her team have shields like that? She got stuck with this dinky circular one.

After he'd tapped the guy twice with his sword, Arlas turned his head to call back to her. "You okay?"

They were both sweaty and splattered with mud, but he was damn handsome with that concerned look. "Yeah, he didn't hit me."

"Good." Arlas blocked an arrow and then leaned into her ear. "Do you see the creek bed back there?"

"Yeah." The creek had all but dried up, but when the spring thaw hit, it'd fill up again.

"Alright, Alete the Ninja. Hop down there and attack them from below." A grin lit up that rugged face, and Jenna returned it.

"Yes, General." She winked.

The thought hadn't even occurred to her, but it should have. Now Jenna was fighting back, jumping up from below the battlefield and "stabbing" her adversaries in the neck with her foam dagger. In the end, the combined forces of Themiscyra and Melberth were victorious. Fighters were patting each other on the back, ready to celebrate.

Jenna was ready for a shower.

"Good job, Alete." A familiar voice made her jump from its nearness.

"Thanks, Arlas."

"Are you staying for the feast tonight?" He put his shield down, leaning on it.

"I am."

Arlas smiled. "I'll see you later, then." As he sauntered off, she pouted inwardly when she realized his garb covered his ass from view.

"Oh, you'll see me, alright." She grinned. Time to go get cleaned up. Jenna had a general to ride.

She marched herself back over to the tent she was sharing with Erin to grab her bag. Erin got there just as she was ready to leave. "Heading to the shower cabin?"

"Hell yes."

"Let me grab my shit and I'll come with you."

"Sure." Jenna was grateful for the guidance. The last thing she needed was to get lost in this maze of teams and tents.

"How do you clean these things off anyway?" She'd borrowed armor from her new roommate, and both women were now covered in mud. Even the tight spandex shorts she wore under the faux leather skirt were crusted with it.

"Honestly, it's easy to wipe them off after the mud dries. Spray the inside with vodka to get the sweat smell out, and you're good to go." Erin shrugged. "I'll hang them in my car so we don't track any more mud inside the tent."

"Vodka? Really?" Jenna asked, one brow raised.

"Yup." Erin nodded. "Don't ask me how it works; my dancer friend told me about it."

"Alright." The garb wasn't Jenna's, anyway.

There was a line of people on either side of the shower cabin. Men on one side, women on another. Gray clouds swirled overhead, and Jenna prayed she'd get clean before the rain started.

When she finally got inside, she took what had to be the fastest shower of her life. The line had only gotten longer while they waited their turn, everyone having the same idea: Get clean before the feast.

Erin laid the armor out over a tarp in the backseat of her car while Jenna put her things away in the tent. Then they made their way from the camp all the way to the other side, where people were piling wood in preparation for a big bonfire. A circle of people with drums sat off to the side, women in long skirts with hip belts dripping with coins standing around.

"What's up with the Romani cosplayers?"

"Hmm?" Erin looked where she pointed. "Oh, those are belly dancers. Not Romani."

"I thought you said it was a party."

"It is! But we can't exactly set up a DJ in the woods." Erin giggled at her.

The bonfire sparked to life, and the smell of roasted meats wafted through the air. Her eyes roamed the campgrounds. Nothing looked out of place. No one looked familiar. Jenna breathed a sigh of relief; she was safe for now. She didn't want to wait for the main course. Instead, she set herself up with a hot dog roasting fork and cooked her own dinner.

"I can't decide if this is a good time to talk to you or not."

Arlas's voice behind her made her jump.

"Why wouldn't it be?"

"Well, you've got a rather phallic-looking object roasting on a stick. Makes a man concerned for his own wiener."

Jenna snorted. "You're in no danger." Her gaze took in his freshly showered appearance. The tight black t-shirt showed off his biceps and his jeans hung low on trim hips. "I just like my wieners hot." She winked.

He grinned and nodded at the fork in her hand. "That one's on fire."

Shit. Her head snapped to pay attention to her dinner, now charred within an inch of its life. "Nothing a little ketchup won't cover up."

He laughed, and Jenna felt a little twist deep in her gut. The man was a walking temptation, and she was dying to bring this flirtation to its logical conclusion. But the condiments table was several yards away, and she was starving. She put some sway in her hips as she stalked back over to it, setting up her hot dog the way she wanted. When she turned back around, Arlas was watching her. She took advantage and held his gaze while licking up the excess ketchup from her dog. She didn't miss the shudder as his eyes blazed at her. With a flirtatious lick of her lips, Jenna turned back around and devoured her hot dog as a low beat started to ring throughout the clearing.

She wiped her hands on a napkin as more beats joined the first, combining to create a heady music that called to one and all. A primal sound, interrupted by yips and cries of joy as the jingle of the belly dancers' coins sang a melody. As the flames of the bonfire climbed higher, Jenna found herself lured toward the circle of stones to where the revelers had gathered on the other side. Firelight made the dancers glow as they circled the drummers in their center. The feast had truly begun.

Her hips swayed with the beat as she watched, when a spicy, male scent floated to her nostrils, and a familiar voice purred in her ear. "Care to dance, Alete?"

"I don't really dance, Arlas," she said, casting her eyes behind her to see his scruffy, firm jaw outlined in red and orange light.

"Want to watch them together, then?"

"Sure."

He took her by the hand and led her into the shadows, leaning against a tree with her in front of him. She shivered at the loss of heat.

"I'll keep you warm." Pulling her hips back to meet his, she felt his erection at her ass.

"Is that for the dancers?"

"No, that's from watching you shake your cute little ass." He growled, and Jenna felt her panties grow damp.

"Watch them," he spoke in her ear. "Watch them and shake that ass just for me, little Amazon."

"What's in it for me, General?" She crossed her arms over her chest and stood perfectly still, despite the way she wanted to sway.

"I'll give you a night you'll never forget." His fingers dug into her hips. God, that voice had her nipples hard and aching behind her bra. "Tell me I can touch you, and I'll show you just how good I can make your night."

She shuddered just from his breath on her ear. "Make me come without exposing me, and I'm yours."

"Challenge accepted, little Amazon." His tongue swirled over the cartilage of her ear, then his lips traveled down her neck. "Don't forget to dance."

She let the rhythm move her hips, grinding into his crotch as she watched the dancers' skirts swirl in the night. Arlas's hands dipped below the hem of her t-shirt, then one rose to cup her breast, tweaking the nipple through her bra. The other slipped into her jeans, into her panties, to cup her mound.

"Christ, Alete, you're drenched." His finger began to circle her clit as the other hand reached inside her bra to pet her neglected breast. "I wanna suck these titties while you come on my hand."

His words pulled a groan from her chest as her hips swayed tighter against his body. Two thick fingers dove into her pussy and she popped the button on her jeans to give him more room to work. Her head fell back against his shoulder as he drove her higher and higher. He pinched each nipple in turn.

"Come for me, little Amazon." When he put just the right pressure on her clit, every muscle went tense, her body jerking in his hold. Her eyes closed as she came with a gasp.

As she came back to her body, she realized moans surrounded them in the woods.

"You don't have to hold back."

Jenna shook her head. "I've never..."

Pulling his hands free from her clothes, Arlas turned her around. She could barely make out his face in the darkness. "It's okay. I don't mind you saving those sexy little sounds for me." His teeth glinted with starlight as he grinned. "Just promise you'll get loud when we get to my tent."

"Let's go." She reached out and grabbed hold of his dick in his pants as he hissed. "There's something I need to take care of."

"I'm tempted to throw you over my shoulder."

"Cavemen don't get blow jobs from Amazons." She released his dick after a quick squeeze and buttoned her pants again. The man was packing, and she couldn't wait.

"It'd make getting to my tent faster, though." He produced a small flashlight on a key ring and pointed it at the ground while he led them away from the festivities.

She bit her lip. "Would you settle for a piggyback ride?"

He crouched down almost immediately. "Hop on, little Amazon."

"Save a horse, ride a general."

Arlas reached around to squeeze her ass as he lifted her into the air. "Promises, promises."

She clung to his shoulders as he jogged through the woods. Every step he took rubbed the seam of her pants over her clit, ratcheting her arousal right back up. She breathed a sigh of relief when a circle of tents appeared in the light of his flashlight. He headed for a bright blue one, kneeling and unzipping the door just as the skies opened up and rain began to pour. Shrieks from the revelers still at the party barely reached their ears. Roger just shook his head.

"I keep telling them the drum circle is a rain dance."

Jenna threw her head back and laughed as he rolled her off his back and on to an open sleeping bag. The harsh light of a camping lantern filled the space, giving them an eerie glow.

"That mud is gonna suck, though."

Arlas smirked. "Who said you were leaving before morning?"

Jenna rose to a sitting position and carefully took off her boots to keep herself from tracking mud into his sleeping area. "You going to give me a reason to stay that long?"

He let off another growl, and Jenna knew there would be no salvaging her underwear. "I have plenty of stamina for you, little Amazon."

For once, Jenna felt like her old self; the person she'd been before she got into the bullshit lifestyle she'd adopted just to survive. She wasn't sure if it was the game or the man in front of her, but she was going to grasp the bull by both horns and refuse to let go.

"Good, because you made me a promise back there that I want you to make good on." With that, Jenna whipped off her t-shirt and watched as his eyes fell right to her breasts. It wasn't even one of her good bras, just plain white cotton. She shucked off her jeans as he started to strip, and she had to discretely check her chin for drool. The man was muscular in a way that said he did some kind of labor. His six-pack wasn't sharply defined in the way a gym rats would be, but it was still there.

"You have tatts?" Arlas murmured at her.

"Mm-hmm," was her only response as her hands roamed all that warm, firm skin.

His hands meandered over her body too, tracing over the birdcage on her left shoulder, and then he pushed her onto her back on the sleeping bag.

"Is that a... popsicle?"

She had to laugh. He'd found the classic patriotic red, white, and blue popsicle on her inner thigh. That one had hurt, but it had been worth it. It pointed directly at her pussy, like she was melting it. It was her giant middle finger to her wannabe-patriot father. Then Arlas's tongue was on it, and her laughter died away.

"That's not where I want licked."

He grinned, sliding his tongue over the ink. "Coulda fooled me."

Why were his boxers still on?

"Aren't you going to take the rest of your clothes off?"

"All in good time, little Amazon. I promised you something, and I mean to deliver it first." Then he was pulling her plain cotton panties down with his teeth!

All Jenna could do was groan as his fingers circled her entrance, toying with her, teasing her. Arlas pulled her underwear the rest of the way off, and then rose above her, his fingers still playing around. The rain smacked against the tent harder, and she heard voices as his teammates returned to camp.

"Don't get shy now, Alete. Let's make my teammates jealous." Then those wicked lips latched onto her nipple as his fingers plunged inside.

Chapter 3

His little Amazon's moans rang through the night. There would be no doubt in anyone's mind what was happening in Roger's tent as he swirled his thumb over her clit and his tongue over her nipple. His fingers started thrusting as he switched back and forth between her tits. They were just barely too big to fit entirely in his mouth. He felt her pussy clench around him as he sucked, and licked, and fucked her on two fingers. After her second orgasm of the night, he added a third finger as she squirmed.

"One more, baby, one more, then you can ride this cock all you want."

Whimpers poured from Alete's throat, but her hips started thrusting back against his hand. He nibbled at the place where her shoulder met her neck and felt her shiver under him.

"You like that, huh?" he murmured, more to himself than to her. Then he latched on and sucked hard. A cry. Then her hips started fucking herself on his hand in earnest, her nails digging into his scalp and pushing him back down to her glorious tits. No complaints from him.

He sucked and bit those breasts and nipples until he knew she'd see his marks in the morning, and for several days after. Usually, he didn't get territorial over his conquests, but something about this woman made him want to piss in a circle around her, or tattoo "Roger was here" on her abdomen.

When her inner walls fluttered over his fingers and she cried out again, he slowly brought her down from the high. He sucked his fingers into his mouth and moaned when her flavor exploded on his tongue while Alete caught her breath.

"You still with me?"

Her only answer was a grin. And then he was flat on his back, facing the ceiling of his tent. "It's my turn now, General," she purred, and peeled his pants and boxers down.

Oh. Oh, the hot dog wasn't just a tease. Her hot little tongue swirled over his cock and made him freeze. Before she could swallow him down, he grabbed her leg and pulled it over his head, his thumb skimming over a rough, round bump on the back of her thigh. His lust-addled brain skipped over the obvious bullet wound scar. He wasn't interested in swapping stories tonight.

"Sit on my face, Alete. I'm still hungry." He yanked those hips down and pressed his tongue into her clit, sucking it into his mouth even as the heat of her mouth surrounded his dick.

He ate her like a starving man, holding off his own climax until she shook over his head with another. Before she could get him too close, he lifted her tiny curvy body off his. "Condom in my pants pocket."

She grabbed his jeans and found the foil packet quickly. Turning to look at him, he was pleased to see Alete's skin flushed with satisfaction. "Not coming anywhere but that pussy, so if you want to drive, now's your chance."

Taking the hint, she rolled the condom down his length and straddled him. Then the little tease hovered over his dick, barely letting the tip dip into the heaven between her legs. He grabbed onto her hips with a growl. "I'm a patient man, Alete, but I do have limits."

"I'm a little nervous about that pipe you had in your pants. It's intimidating."

His grip softened as he stroked her soft, pale skin. "That's why I insisted on all those orgasms first, little Amazon. I don't want to hurt you."

She nodded and then took her time to sink gloriously down onto his shaft. Pausing as his balls met her ass, he let her get used to his girth.

"Fuuuuuuuuck," she groaned.

He had to agree. "Move when you're ready, baby."

Slowly, she circled her hips, and he nearly shot his load like an untried virgin. As she got more comfortable, she started lifting herself up and down his shaft. Soon she was riding him hard, and when his balls tightened, Roger knew he wouldn't last long. He slipped his thumb down over her mound and rubbed circles over her clit. That did it. Her pussy spasmed around him as her climax took over, and then Roger grasped her hips and thrust up into her, a grunting, bucking bronco as his orgasm drew up from his toes and shot through his cock. Their cries mingled in the night, Alete collapsing onto his chest even as the aftershocks of her orgasm pulsed around his shaft, still buried in her. They caught their breath as the rain pounded the tent.

"Damn." Her breath tickled his neck.

"Damn is right," he answered. "Let me take care of the condom."

She rolled off him as he slid out from under her, tied off the condom, and tossed it into his trash bag. By the time he turned around, she was snoring on his pillow. He smiled at the tiny sound, and slipped back into the sleeping bag, killing the lantern as she dozed. Roger didn't normally do sleepovers, but he couldn't kick her out in the rain. Besides, this way he could wake her for another round.

JENNA SLID OUT FROM under the arm holding her down as soon as she awoke. It was dark out still, but the faint chirp of the earliest birds reached her ears. She dressed hastily, mostly by feel, and stepped into her shoes just as she unzipped the tent flap for a bit of light. Slipping through the small opening, she zipped it back into place. Good to know her stealth skills were still intact, even if she didn't use them anymore.

She padded quietly through Melberth's camp, their members still asleep. She made her way across the other camps back to Themyscira, and her roommate's tent.

Erin was packing up when she arrived, giving her a smirk. "How was he?"

"Glorious," Jenna said with a stretch. "I needed that." Erin tossed the last of their gear into her sedan and opened the driver's side door.

"Breakfast is on me. There's this little diner on the way back home."

"Sounds perfect, Roomie." She hopped into the passenger's seat and leaned the seat back. "I'm going to nap till we get there."

"Didn't get much sleep with Arlas, huh?" Erin smirked.

"You know it." Jenna was deliciously sore in all the right places, but her chest ached too. She rubbed her hand over her sternum. That was new. But it didn't matter if she regretted running away in the early morning — her roommate needed to work today, which meant they had to get back to Baltimore. Besides, attachments could still get her killed.

Her last relationship had ended when her ex "borrowed" some of her equipment without asking. She'd been on a job and had to find an alternative way down from the ceiling when her repelling gear wasn't in her bag where she kept it. This had been years ago, back when she first found herself in her former life. At the time, it hadn't been six months since her parents had cut her off and she'd had to find her own way to make money without a college degree. When he said he'd "borrowed" it to go rock climbing, Jenna cut him loose — because he'd been on a date with another woman. But it had taught her a valuable lesson. She didn't let anyone get close after that.

And now, with her former employer certainly pissed at her disappearing act, it was even more dangerous. If she got attached to someone, then they could be used against her. Or get caught in the crossfire.

Jenna squashed the pang of guilt knowing she'd placed Erin in harm's way as her roommate, but she hadn't had a choice. She had to establish herself in Baltimore before trying to lease an apartment under her new identity as Amber Smith. No landlord would rent to someone without an employment history. But Erin, working for the police department as a dispatcher, would protect her. At least, she hoped so. Jenna told herself she was done using people. That she'd get away from Erin as soon as possible. Her ex-employer wasn't stupid, but he also wasn't patient. If he did find Jenna hiding behind Erin, he'd shoot first and just hide the additional body.

She watched the highway fly along outside her window as Taylor Swift sang about James Dean and red lips on the radio. Her stomach growled just as Erin took an exit to the right. The ramp let them out a few hundred feet from the gravel parking lot of a classic diner. It had the silver bullet exterior, a neon "Open" sign in the window, and the scents rolling through the summer breeze reminded Jenna of lazy Saturday mornings when her parents' cook made them a leisurely brunch.

A sign told them to seat themselves. Erin and Jenna slid into a booth upholstered in turquoise vinyl. Laminated menus greeted them from behind the napkin holder. Jenna flipped her coffee mug right side up and perused the diner's extensive breakfast menu. A busy waitress with a full tray sidled up to their table and filled their mugs.

"I'll be right with you, girls."

"Thanks," Erin responded for them. "They have really good pancakes here."

"That sounds perfect." When the server came back around, she introduced herself as Louise and took their orders.

"Thanks for inviting me out." Jenna doctored her coffee and closed her eyes as she took a sip.

"You're welcome. I'm glad you had fun."

Well, fighting like that wasn't exactly what Jenna considered fun, but the after party had been.

On their way to the campground, they'd talked about mundane, superficial things. Jenna tried to steer the conversation away from herself as much as possible. Hopefully, Erin wouldn't notice the way she avoided talking about her old life.

"Where did you grow up, Amber?" Her roommate asked as she poured the cream into her mug.

"Out west. We moved around." That wasn't entirely a lie. They had moved when she was little, from her father's hometown to Santa Fe, the capital where he served.

Louise returned with their food, and Erin broke off her line of questioning. Talk about service. "Here you go, ladies. Enjoy!"

Fluffy pancakes with a side of egg and sausage lay on the plate in front of her. "Smells delicious!" She poured the syrup and dug in, all too aware of their time constraints. Erin was attacking her omelet with gusto.

"How are we on gas? I can fill her up for you."

Erin waved her off. "We're fine to get home. I want to hop in a shower with decent water pressure before my shift."

"Bathroom's all yours when we get there." Jenna looked down at her vibrating phone. "Looks like someone called off and they want to see if I can pick up a shift."

"You didn't get much sleep last night. You going to be okay?"

"Yeah, I'll grab a nap before I go in." She texted her boss back, confirming she could come in.

"So," Erin spoke low, leaning in across the table. "Are the rumors true?"

"About Arlas?" After their first meeting, she'd asked Erin about Arlas. Jenna recalled the way Erin had held her hands apart, indicating he was gifted. "I didn't have my measuring tape." Something irked her about her roommate discussing his cock. For some reason, she wanted to keep that information to herself.

"It's probably better to leave it a mystery," Erin sighed. "He's never looked my way, so best not to think about what I'm missing. It would be weird now that you've been with him, anyway."

Jenna lifted her coffee mug to hide the snarl she was fighting. Ugh, what the hell was wrong with her? She probably just needed that nap.

After scarfing their food down, Erin paid the check at the front counter and they got back on the road. The trip back to Baltimore passed with no more conversation, the radio filling the silence between them.

It was still early when they pulled onto their crowded street, but thankfully, someone pulled out of a space close to the apartment just as they did. Erin slid into the space expertly, then Jenna groaned as she unfolded herself from the seats. Her stiff muscles were another sign she was getting older. That had been part of her reason for leaving her old job; it was way too physical for someone in her thirties.

"I'll help you unpack."

"Just grab one end of the tent."

After Erin had the door open, they each slung a bag on their shoulder and marched the tent in its case through, one of them at each end. The door shut behind Jenna and Erin locked the car with her remote.

"Enjoy your shower, and have a good shift."

"You, too. Oh, do you want me to pick you up after you're done?"

"I'll take the bus."

"It's no trouble; and if you end up closing, they won't be running."

"Good point. Yeah, if you don't mind."

"It's not a problem. I have a raid I'm staying up for, anyway."

Leave it to Jenna to rent a room from a total nerd. She'd found out shortly after moving in that Erin played an online role-playing game along with the LARPing. But it worked out in her best interest, since Erin could pick her up tonight.

While Erin took the world's shortest shower, in her own words, Jenna unpacked her bag and threw her dirty clothes in her hamper. It was just a pop-up one like she'd used in college, but it was better than the floor. Maybe if she got to a place where she could stick around, she'd get a nice wicker one her mother would have approved of.

Jenna might have chafed under the constant need to keep up appearances, but she'd never accuse the governor's wife of having poor taste. What would her parents think of her now? Camping and beating people with foam swords while working as a bartender in a dive bar was not the image the O'Malleys had wanted to cultivate for their daughter. No, they had expected her to graduate from Dad's alma mater with honors, with a degree in political science, then go on to law school. Or marry the right politician's son and have babies while she turned a blind eye to his mistresses.

Never in a million years. Jenna hated politics and what it had done to her family. She'd never subject a child to that life. And now she didn't dare get close to anyone for fear of her worst decision coming back to bite her in the ass.

Ugh, she needed a hobby. A wandering mind caused too much unpleasantness.

"Amber, I'm leaving! Text me what time to pick you up, okay?"

"Roger that! Have a good shift!"

The door slammed shut and Jenna stripped and tossed her clothes with the rest, then headed straight for the shower and her pre-shift nap.

Chapter 4

ONE MONTH LATER, ROGER leaned back in his computer chair, cleared his throat, and raised his shot glass to his lips. "For Eddie," he toasted.

"Cheers, brother." Sam raised his on the screen, and they poured the liquor to the back of their throats.

He didn't get to connect with Sam much anymore since they both split from the Army. Roger had moved back to Baltimore, and Sam went home to Colorado. His friend had been the intelligence specialist for his squad. Sam's skills meant the FBI, specifically their cybercrime division, had recruited him. Between their schedules and the time zone difference, even a video chat was difficult to organize.

"Man, that goes down nice. You're spoiling me."

"It's the least I could do after your help last year."

Once Sam had heard that Nadia had been kidnapped, he'd jumped on her trail. Without his connections, Roger never could have tracked his baby sister's cell and rescued her. Sam had refused any payment for his time, saying he was just happy to help a brother. He'd sent him a bottle of Knob Creek Bourbon, anyway.

"I still owe you that favor, by the way."

"Hopefully, I never have to call it in."

They started shooting the shit about work. Roger's latest job at the jewelry store had come to a close, and he found himself at loose ends. Sam complained about an organized crime case he'd been roped into assisting.

"They call this guy The Sly Fox. He never leaves a trail, never shows up on camera, and never gets caught."

"What's he steal?"

"Gems, primarily. The big, pricey ones you find in museums."

"Wouldn't they have good security?"

"You would think, right? But every time something goes missing, the cameras are tampered with." Sam gave him a knowing look.

That explained why they'd called Sam in. "He's got a hacker friend."

"And *that's* why I got sucked into this. They figure if they can find the hacker, they can find the Fox. There's only one problem."

"What's that?"

Sam poured himself another shot. "He hasn't stolen anything in months. They're champing at the bit, waiting for him to show himself. And I'm left sitting on my hands looking like an idiot."

"You could always come work for me." Roger eyed Sam over the edge of his second shot. Usually, he got a resounding "No." This time, Sam seemed to consider it.

"If you get any jobs that sound like you need me, you let me know. I can moonlight if I'm careful."

"You should come to Baltimore. Check out the bay. We have much better winters than Denver."

At that, Sam snorted. "I'm pretty sure Alaska gets less snow than we do."

"Only because they have it year-round."

Sam chuckled. "I'll think about it. I'm due for some vacation time here soon. We can hang out."

"Just like old times." Roger sipped at the liquor in his glass.

"Except I'm too damn old to go picking up chicks in bars."

"Who says?"

"Women only got with me for the uniform, Hunt, you know that. I can't talk to them for shit."

Roger shook his head. "Whatever you say, brother." Before he could change the subject, Roger's business phone rang.

"Looks like we'll have to cut this short." Sam set his glass down.

"I'll call you back, man. This shouldn't take long."

Roger reluctantly ended the video call as he picked up the cell he kept for his security business. "Hunt Security, this is Roger."

"Mr. Hunt, my name is Patrick O'Malley. I'm the governor of New Mexico."

He stole a look at the clock on his laptop. Well, it was still business hours in New Mexico, so that made sense. "What can I do for you, sir?"

A chuckle came down the line. "Ah, that's the old army training right there, isn't it? I have a very important job and I have hand-selected you to do it. There have been death threats made against my family, and I need a bodyguard for my daughter."

"I'm honored, Governor. But I'm not sure why you wouldn't want to hire a security firm closer to home."

O'Malley's chair creaked in the background. "Well, you see, my daughter and I haven't spoken in a while. But given the situation, I hired a private investigator to find her. He tracked her down to Baltimore. I have the address and everything."

"Are you sure it's her, sir?"

"Oh, I'm sure. She's changed her hair, but I'd know my Jenna anywhere. I want you specifically on this job, Mr. Hunt. No one else at your firm."

Roger didn't feel like explaining he still hadn't managed to hire anyone. "That won't be a problem."

"She needs guarding twenty-four-seven until the election is over in November. I'll pay you weekly until the job is over." The old man went on to name a ridiculous amount of money. Roger's eyes nearly popped out of his head. He stood to make a year's worth of revenue in one month from this job. Not to mention the good reference an elected official would make.

"Why don't you send me the information and I can take it from there?" He rattled off his email address.

"The password for the file is 'Party.'" An email notification popped up on Roger's laptop. "And by the way, any additional expenses you have for this job, forward me a receipt. I'll reimburse you."

"Will do." Roger had already lost himself in the file. The governor's daughter was a knockout. The photo in the file was dated from a decade ago at some event with her parents. Copper-red hair cascaded down her back. An emerald cocktail dress hugged her petite curves. He would have loved to feel those sky-high heels digging into his back.

But he hated the fake-ass smile she wore. The last thing he wanted to do was spend time around some pampered princess who probably only went to college for her MRS degree. However, the governor had named an amount that ensured he'd take the job.

The recent photos, taken by the PI, showed a woman walking down the sidewalk with black hair, her face covered by a large pair of sunglasses.

"I'll go over first thing in the morning, sir."

Patrick hemmed and hawed. "I should warn you. She may not be very agreeable, Mr. Hunt."

"Please call me Roger. Mr. Hunt is my father."

"Roger," he replied. "If my daughter gives you any trouble, I want you to call me at this number." He rattled off another phone number, which Roger scribbled down. "That is my private cell phone. I don't care what time it is here, you call me. Like I said, we haven't spoken in a long time, and I don't believe she'll agree easily."

"Do the threats mention her?"

A beat passed. "By name."

Shit. This girl was in danger, and Roger couldn't let her turn him away. Both for her sake and his.

Another notification sound rang from his computer.

"I've sent over half of the first week's pay. That should get you started."

"Thank you for your business, sir. I will do my best."

"I would expect nothing less from a Green Beret. Have a good night, Roger."

It seemed the governor had done his homework. Roger didn't discuss his military specialty on the website. Which meant he'd pulled records. He didn't know whether to be creeped out or honored.

Roger said his goodbyes and ended the call. Then, as promised, he rang Sam again. Sam didn't pick up, so he sent him a message over Discord.

> I just got a month-long bodyguard gig for some society princess. Wish me luck.

The next morning, Roger packed a few days of clothes into a duffel bag. He'd prefer to put her up at his place with his state-of-the-art cameras. But if she was as stubborn about this as her father insinuated, he needed to be prepared to stay at her apartment.

He jumped into his trusty Silverado and rumbled down his long gravel driveway. Roger liked that his place was far enough from the road for privacy. His sister liked to needle him about getting it paved, but he'd rather not encourage just anyone to come over. That was half the point of him buying it.

Heading into West Baltimore, he ended up parking a few blocks from the address Patrick had sent him. Red brick rowhouses lined the street, and parking was a nightmare. An old jalopy sat outside the house number he'd been given.

After one mistaken knock, he discovered what the doors didn't convey. He was looking for number fourteen and a *half*. Which meant that little white door at the bottom of the stairs.

What kind of society princess lived in a basement?

He jogged down the cracked cement stairs, refusing to hold the railing that threatened to give him tetanus. Then he knocked with the folder in hand.

His jaw about hit the floor when the door opened inward.

"Alete?"

Chapter 5

HOW THE FUCK HAD her one-night stand from that crazy LARP event found her address? "Arlas?"

Erin called out from the kitchen. "Amber, who is it?"

"You're not going to believe this..." Jenna held the door open and gestured for Arlas to come in. "Arlas, how did you find me?"

"We better go over real names or this is going to get confusing, fast." Their guest said as Erin came into view. "I'm Roger Hunt."

"Erin Healy." Erin held out her hand, which he shook.

"I'm Amber Smith." Jenna held her hand out, giving him her fake name. Before he shook it, he opened a strange folder and checked something inside. Then Roger gave her a scrutinizing look.

This was not the look of a man who wanted another roll in the hay. Roger squinted at her and cocked his head. Then he crossed his arms and shut the door behind him. The lock clicked shut. His very presence in their tiny basement apartment emphasized how short the ceiling was. Jenna found herself backing up into her hallway as he advanced on her.

"That's not your real name."

"Of course it's her real name," Erin answered, indignant on her behalf.

His cold gaze never left Jenna's, and her stomach flipped. Her throat went dry, and she knew she'd been made.

"Why did you give your roommate a fake name, Jenna?"

Jenna broke their stare-down and wiped her clammy hands on her jeans.

"Amber, what's he talking about?"

Swallowing her pride, she knew she had to control the damage. And she was going after the idiot that sold her the new identity as soon as she ran again.

"I told you, my name is Amber."

And denial is just a river in Egypt.

Roger cocked an eyebrow, and Jenna crossed her arms over her chest. "That's not what my client says."

Erin furrowed her brows. "Client? What are you talking about?"

"I run Hunt Security, and the governor of New Mexico contacted me last night to hire a bodyguard for his daughter, who lives in Baltimore." Roger opened the manila folder and showed it to them. "He said he hired a private investigator to find her and gave me this address."

Jenna gulped. Inside the folder was a profile on her, as well as a photo from the last event her father had dragged her to before he cut her off.

"I told you, I'm Amber Smith." She'd paid a lot of money to be able to claim that. Fat lot of good that'd done. If her father could find her this easily, so could the people she was running from.

Roger sighed. "Governor O'Malley warned me you wouldn't want to cooperate. Are you really going to make me prove who you are?"

She kept her face completely neutral, just like when she'd had to go to a campaign event for her father. "Do I need to get my license, Roger?"

An honest-to-goodness growl rattled in the man's throat. And now her panties were wet.

Awkward.

"Licenses can be faked. Hair can be cut and dyed." Roger shoved the photo in her face and pointed at the area where her popsicle tattoo had barely peeked out from under the hem of her short dress. It was in shadow, but she could still see it. "And even if I couldn't see past those things, with *this* tattoo in *that* spot? That is definitely you."

He didn't need to remind her he knew about the tattoo because he'd licked it. Repeatedly.

She was made. And like any other cornered animal, Jenna came out snarling.

"Who the fuck do you think you are? You can't just come waltzing in here and do this to me! I don't care what that over-inflated airship is paying you!" Her nostrils flared and her lips pulled back, baring her teeth as she hauled her short frame up on her tiptoes to get as close to Roger's face as she could, punctuating each word with a poke into his granite chest. "I. Don't. Answer. To. Him."

Roger's unreadable expression only infuriated her further. He grasped her wrist and pulled her hand away from him. "Well, I do, Princess."

Princess? *Princess!* This guy had balls to insinuate she was some helpless damsel in distress. *Her!*

Roger sighed and pulled his cell phone out of his pocket. "Guess I need that number after all."

"What are you doing?" Hadn't he ruined her life enough? Jenna *liked* Baltimore, damn it. She had just started to get the hang of waiting tables and now she had to dig into her savings to run again.

"I'm calling your father. Maybe he can explain what's going on."

The lion, the witch, and the *audacity* of this dick.

"I do *not* talk to my father." Jenna followed him into the living room and perched on the chair across from where Roger had settled on their couch. She crossed her legs and arms simultaneously, unconsciously shielding herself.

Roger answered without looking up from a ringing phone in his palm. "You don't have to talk to him, just listen."

Like *hell*.

Someone picked up the call. "Good morning, Roger." Her father's voice called out over the line.

"Sorry to wake you, Governor O'Malley." Dad's condescending chuckle sent shivers down her shoulders. "I take it she didn't take the news very well."

"She's been living under an assumed name. It was a bit interesting when her roommate didn't know who I was talking about."

"Has she now? Very interesting." He paused. "Is she there?"

"Yes, sir. She's right next to me. You're on speaker."

"Jenna?"

She clenched her jaw. No way did she want to talk to him, especially not after he blew her cover.

Roger waited for her to speak, then sighed at her refusal. "She said she doesn't want to talk to you, so I apologize again. But I thought she might be more understanding of my presence if you explained the situation. If you wouldn't mind."

"I see. One moment." Her father blew out a breath, and she heard her mother's murmur in the background. Then a came rustling of sheets, footsteps, and the click of a door shutting.

"Jenna, I know you're mad, but you have to have protection. I've run into some issues with my campaign."

She rolled her eyes. Of course, this had to do with his precious *campaign*.

"The security team here made me aware of death threats against me and my family. They named you specifically."

Her stomach sank. Just what she needed, another enemy at her back.

"Now, since you don't live here anymore, my security team can't protect you. It's either Mr. Hunt here, or you come back home."

"Fuck, no!" Jenna spat out. "You kicked me out. You don't get to tell me to come back. I've made my *own* damn way without you!"

"Then Roger's going to be your personal bodyguard twenty-four-seven until this election is over."

"This is ridiculous," she muttered, mostly to herself. Where the fuck was she going to put him? He barely fit in their apartment.

"It's not ridiculous. It's very serious," the old coot admonished her.

"That's not..." Jenna slapped her hand over her face. Why did she bother?

"It's only until the election is over, Jenna."

Frustration she hadn't dealt with in ten years choked her. It had always been this way. *Do as you're told, Jenna. Don't make a fuss. You can't wear that, be seen with them,* yadda yadda yadda. She'd thought she'd left all this behind when her parents had cut her off in an attempt to force her to return to their side. She had fought against it then, but today was a different story. Now Roger and Erin were there to witness her shame.

Anger at the attempt to re-tether her after letting her float free for a decade made bile rise in her throat. Roger was a convenient outlet. As usual, her father had delivered his edict and hung up the phone, expecting to be obeyed.

"This is bullshit. I'm not agreeing to this. Besides, we don't have an extra bedroom."

Roger pinched the bridge of his nose, and the light caught a few silver hairs threaded through the brown. For a moment he looked older, and Jenna wondered how old this guy was.

"It would be best if you packed a bag and came to stay with me. I have the space, and I have a state-of-the-art home security system. No one will mess with you there."

"Absolutely not." No way in hell was she moving in with this guy.

Erin spoke up for the first time from where she stood against the wall. "You're welcome to the couch, Roger."

Jenna turned her glare on her roommate. Traitor.

Erin raised both hands in defense. "Look, it sounds serious. At least this way, if anyone tries to get to you, they'll have to go through him."

"I need to see the whole space before I decide what we're doing."

Oh, hell no. "You are not deciding anything. I am not leaving the apartment I pay half the rent for. If you don't like it, you can leave."

"I'm here to do a job, Princess. Which is your security, whether you like it or not. If I can't protect you here, I have to take you somewhere I can."

"You can try," Jenna scoffed. Then she shoved off the chair she and Erin had found on the side of the road last week and stalked back to her bedroom. "I have to get ready for work."

"Where do you work?" Of course, he was following her.

"Urban Roadhouse." She slammed the door in his face and yanked her uniform out of her drawer.

"When you're done in there, I need to assess the security."

"Keep your pants on." That gave Jenna a brilliant idea. She changed out of her jeans into the shortest pair of cut-offs she had. They barely covered her ass. She was going to give him an eyeful on her way out the door.

When she opened the door to find him leaning against her doorjamb, his gaze slid slowly down her body. She could almost feel it, like a caress.

"Don't snoop."

"That's not my job."

She turned to her roommate. "Hey, Erin, I'm closing tonight. Can you pick me up?"

"I guess so."

Jenna ignored Erin's flat tone and the wary look on her face. "Alright, I've got to get to the bus stop."

That brought Roger out of her bedroom. "You can't take the bus!"

"That's what I do, buster."

Erin paused, her gaze pinging between the two of them, then sighed. "I'm off tonight if you want to borrow my car." She was sure Erin thought she was being helpful.

"Either you take her car, or I drive you."

"Fine." Could she give him the slip at work and come back to the apartment to pack? She'd be back on the run before he found a way home.

"Roomie." Erin didn't let go of the keys right away, forcing Jenna to look up at her. The look on her face was hard to read, but she recognized the disappointment in her eyes. "We'll talk tomorrow."

Jenna just nodded. Tomorrow she planned to be gone.

Chapter 6

Riding in the car next to Jenna, Roger swore she was trying to drive him crazy on purpose. Those shorts and that tank top left very little to the imagination and were reminding him of the night they'd spent together.

Which also reminded him of how she left. "You didn't want a second round that night?"

She looked over at him while they waited for a red light. "I didn't have time. Erin had to get home for a daylight shift."

"Pity."

She snorted. "Why, cause you don't do repeats?"

"That's not strictly true."

"That's what the rumors say."

"What else do the rumors say, Jenna?"

"Don't call me that," she hissed.

"Cat's out of the bag, sweetheart."

"Not at work. You call me Amber when we're in public."

"But that's not your name."

She gritted her teeth, and Roger grinned. It was almost as fun to piss her off as it had been to fuck her. Almost.

"The only two people who know who I am in this town are you and my roommate. Trust me when I say we need to keep it that way."

"Alright." He had to admit she had good instincts. Using a fake name might put the people behind the death threats off her trail. "But maybe you should make sure your pants cover that tattoo fully, hmm?" He told himself it was because it was distinctive. Honestly, if it hadn't been for that little detail, she might have convinced him it wasn't her in the photo. But there was also an underlying layer of jealousy; it was true he didn't do repeats in the bedroom, at least not often, and not without a conversation about what no-strings meant. Then why did he want to keep other men from seeing her body when she had it on display?

It had to be his protective instincts. He'd have the same reaction to Nadia dressing that way, although between him, Jon, and Finn, they'd made sure Nadia could hold her own in most situations.

That had to be the reason he wanted to throw a blanket over her legs and drag her back to the apartment. She was under his protection now. Which meant using her fake name, as much as he hated to admit that she was right.

Jenna pulled her roommate's old sedan around to the back of the restaurant. Roger had to assume that's where the employees parked.

"Which section is yours?" He pulled the door open for her to walk through.

"I'll let you know when I find out." She didn't look at him as she walked past the kitchen to the front of the house.

"Hey, Cindy."

"Hi, Amber." A bottle-blonde stood behind the bar, snapping her gum. "You're on the far side today." She eyed Roger like he was a steak. "Who's your friend?"

Jenna scanned the computer screen that must double as cash register and punch clock, then keyed in a code. "He's just hanging out tonight."

Well, Mama taught him to be polite. "Roger," he said, offering his hand. Jenna's coworker, or boss, he wasn't sure, shook it, her gaze crawling over him the whole time. After getting his hand back, he tried to wipe off the slimy feelings she gave him by surreptitiously rubbing his palm on his jeans.

Jenna headed off toward her section of the mostly empty restaurant, the lunch rush not yet begun. He let his gaze wander, cataloging exits and windows, and seated himself in the corner of Jenna's section, where he was both out of the way and had a line of sight to any potential danger. As long as she didn't go back to the kitchen much, he'd be able to keep an eye on her.

When she came to his table, she rolled her eyes. "You're seriously going to camp here the whole time?"

"That's my job," he reminded her. "Do you go back to the kitchen a lot?"

"Not until my break."

"Take your break here, where I can see you."

She shook her head and crossed her arms. "I have to be off the floor or people will get ideas."

"And I have to have eyes on you at all times." He also didn't trust her not to run. "By the way, give me Erin's keys."

"Excuse me?"

He smirked. "Call it insurance. I'll hold on to them until the end of your shift."

"Ugh, fine." She flipped them out of her pocket and smacked them onto the table. "Let me make sure I have this straight. You want me to take my break on the floor where I'm not supposed to and stay out of the kitchen? What if I have to pee? Are you going to follow me into the bathroom?"

Now it was his turn to roll his eyes. It was a good thing the governor was paying as much as he was. Roger wasn't sure who this woman was, but she was totally different from the person he'd met before. He missed his Amazon from the LARP event. "No, I'm not going to follow you into the bathroom."

She huffed. "Well, the staff bathroom is back there, so at some point I'll have to go back." Then she leaned over and hissed, "No one knows about me as long as you keep your mouth shut."

He mimed locking his lips and tossing the key, avoiding looking at her cleavage while he did. "Can I get a water and a burger?"

"Fries okay?"

"Sure." He could use this downtime to get some admin stuff done for the business while keeping an eye out for his charge at the same time.

Jenna's shift passed tortuously slowly. Roger found his gaze glued to her tight, curvy ass in those shorts every time she sauntered by. He glared at more than one man checking her out. During the day, most of them backed off. It was once the sun set that other men merely found him amusing.

After the dinner rush was over, Jenna walked up to his table once more. She'd checked on him through the course of her shift like she would any other patron, although she was decidedly colder to him than she was to other tables. But he wasn't a normal customer, and she knew it.

She handed him his check. "I'm done in a few."

He pulled out his card without reading the total, but she shook her head. "We're not allowed to run cards for friends. Cindy can close out your tab at the bar."

Roger nodded and stood, shaking the pins and needles out of his legs. He'd been sitting there too long. "Alright, I'll meet you at the back door."

Jenna shook her head again. "We're leaving out the front. I got told off about non-employees in the back."

"Got it." He should probably apologize, but Roger couldn't really say he was sorry for doing his job.

Cindy did indeed close out his tab at the bar, but not without eyeing him up again. Usually, he wouldn't mind, but something about her made him squeamish. It had to be because he was on the clock. It couldn't have anything to do with Jenna.

"Will we be seeing you around?"

"Most likely." He pocketed his receipt, then looked around for Jenna. She stood at the front door with her bag on her shoulder, scowling at him. He strode over, then held the door for her. "After you."

"Thanks," she bit out. She stalked back around the building to where she'd parked her roommate's car. He grabbed her arm just as she went to open the door.

"What now? You're not driving, Roger."

The way she growled was downright adorable, but he was too smart to tell her that. Holding back his smile, Roger pulled her hand back from the car. "I need to be sure it wasn't tampered with, *Amber.*" He growled, reminding her why he was here. His thorough inspection of the vehicle turned up nothing but a loose cap on one tire.

"Can I go home *now*?" His charge whined. "My feet are killing me."

"It's safe now, Princess." He grinned as she threw herself into the car with a huff. Maybe this job was going to be fun.

She was silent on the trip home. While he didn't want to rule out that she might be giving him the cold shoulder, it was possible she was just tired of being social. Roger decided to let her stew in silence.

When they got back to the apartment, Jenna parked down the street and marched quickly to the front door.

He raced ahead under the glow of the streetlights to catch up.

"Slow down."

She crossed her arms and spun to face him. "Come on, Roger. I've had a long day and I want to go to bed."

He scoffed. He'd had a long day, too, damn it. And he would still be working when they went through that door.

Roger gave the door a quick glance to be sure there were no signs of a break-in, then nodded to let her know it was safe. Jenna threw open the door and stalked inside, carrying her purse through to her bedroom.

"I'm going to shower."

"Goodnight." Roger pulled his duffel bag up from where it had landed next to the couch. Erin must have laid out the extra pillow and blanket for him.

Exhaustion hit him as the water turned on, and he dug out a pair of lounge pants. He left his boots under the coffee table and changed quickly while Jenna was busy. Then he thumbed through the messages on his phone. Jonathon had called hours ago, but hadn't left a message. Roger decided to text him instead.

Roger: Hey man, you still up? I couldn't talk earlier because I got a bodyguard gig.

Easy enough. Roger listened as the shower shut off, and the opening and closing of doors that indicated Jenna was safely ensconced back in her room. He'd checked and the window in her room had bars across it to prevent intruders. At least the landlord had done that right. Tomorrow, he would install the security cameras he'd stashed in the truck.

He dialed Jon's number and put the phone to his ear.

"Joe's Sex Shop, come again and again and again."

Roger groaned. "You're going to get in trouble with that line one day."

He could hear the sheepish grin on his brother's face. "At least I get laid, old man."

"You're not the only one, Navy boy. I just don't feel a need to talk about it."

"Fine, fine."

Maybe now they could get down to business. "Listen, I'm on the clock twenty-four-seven right now. Make it quick."

Jon let out a whistle. "I hope you're getting paid well."

"Don't worry about me. What's up?"

A moment of silence on the other end made the hair on the back of his neck prickle. "Finn's going to the sandpit."

"From Okinawa?"

"Yeah, his unit got pulled for active duty."

"Are you supposed to be telling me this?"

"He already called Mom and Dad. I'm just letting you know he's got a few weeks' worth of leave and he's flying in soon to spend time at home."

Roger rubbed a hand over his face. Jon had earned himself a nice safe desk job in the Navy, and he'd retired from the Special Forces himself. But Finn, the youngest of the Hunt boys, was still active in the Marines. And he was a decorated sniper. Mentally, Roger kicked himself. He should have seen this coming.

"Who's telling Nadia?"

"Mom got that job."

"Good. At least she won't be blindsided." Their baby sister was six years younger than Finn and sixteen younger than Roger. The first time he'd been deployed she'd been in preschool and hadn't fully understood the implications. Once she was old enough to worry, she'd been a force of nature. His CO had called her "the little beret" on more than one occasion.

And Finn was the brother she felt closest to.

"Anyway, make sure you come to Sunday dinner when he's here. Dad invoked boys' night and Caleb's coming, too. Nadia can keep Mom company."

"If it's in the next couple of weeks, I don't know. I can't leave my charge. My client was adamant about her safety."

"What's the problem?"

Roger blew out a breath and tried to decide how much he could tell Jon. "A politician received death threats that named his daughter specifically, and he hired me to be her bodyguard. He told her it was either this or go home and she definitely doesn't want to do *that*."

"Got it. I'll let Mom know to set an extra place. You know she's going to make enough food for a whole platoon, anyway."

"Yeah, no kidding." Judy Hunt had worried about each of them every time they announced they were going to enlist. Only Jon had gone to officer school. Finn had a few more years to go before he could retire from military life. Roger wondered to himself if he could hire him when he finally left the Marines. Maybe he'd bounce early if he knew there was something waiting for him. They had worked well together when a small-time thug kidnapped Nadia the previous year. With a sniper on staff, he could do other hostage extraction jobs.

He filed the idea away for safekeeping. While Finn was stateside, he'd try to get him alone and talk to him.

"Alright, send me details once you have them. As long as she's not working, I'll be there."

"She's got death threats against her and she's still going to work?"

"I can't really discuss this, you know."

"Fair enough. You're probably in her space right now."

Roger grunted an affirmative.

"Alright, get some sleep. Sounds like you're going to need to stay rested with this one."

"You too, brother. Night."

"Night."

Roger plugged his phone into the charger he'd brought and made up his bed. It wasn't even a full-size sofa, just a loveseat. Even though he was the shorter brother, he was still six feet tall. This was going to suck.

Chapter 7

WHEN JENNA WOKE UP way too early the next morning, she wanted to blame her bodyguard for putting her on edge. But that would be a lie. Her dreams had been plagued by two villains; the henchmen of her former boss, and a shapeless one she couldn't see. But she was good at hiding her emotions, having had lots of practice. It would take more than a nightmare to get her to admit she was shaken by the threats her father had received. And her gut said to take them seriously. That's why she told herself she hadn't followed through on her plan to ditch Roger last night. It had nothing to do with him taking the key.

She scrubbed the sleep out of her eyes and rolled out of bed. Throwing a hoodie over her sleep tank, she meandered out to the open-plan kitchen to get coffee. What she saw woke her up faster than an espresso.

Roger was doing push-ups in her living room. Shirtless. Sweat glistened along the muscles of his back, and Jenna's mouth went dry. Then he stood up, and she caught sight of his front. She'd forgotten how ripped the guy was. She hadn't had enough time to appreciate it during their night together. He wiped his towel over his head, which raised his arms and made his athletic shorts slide down, showing off that V that made her stupid. And she knew from experience that it pointed at a very impressive cock.

He dropped the towel, and her gaze flew back to his face, which smirked at her. "Done gawking?"

She shook her head and muttered, "Coffee," like it would explain everything. "You want some?"

"Coffee?"

"Yes."

"Later. I need to hydrate." Then he was right next to her, pouring himself a glass of water, his biceps gleaming. The coffee sputtered, and she watched his Adam's apple bob as he drank half the glass in one go. He threw his towel around his neck, then turned to face her.

"I'm going to hit the shower. Don't leave the apartment."

Right. Bodyguard. Jenna stared at the mug of wakefulness on the counter. Her brain came online when the bathroom door shut. She added her sugar and creamer, then made her way back to her room.

Before she could make it there, Erin's door opened. "Hey, got a minute?"

"Don't you work today?" Her roommate was still wearing pajamas.

"I have the evening shift." She walked deeper into her room, clearly expecting Jenna to follow.

Jenna shut the door behind her, then perched on the bed while Erin settled into her desk chair.

She scrubbed a hand over her face, her mouth in a line. Jenna had never seen her look this serious. "Look, I thought about kicking you out because you lied to me." When Jenna's stomach dropped, Erin raised her hand. "I won't do that, because I'm not an asshole, but I need to know. Why did you lie about who you were?" She cocked her head to the side. "I thought we were going to be friends."

Shit. Growing up as a politician's daughter, Jenna had never really had friends, only people whose parents wanted them to play together. Even as a toddler, she'd been used for political gain. At three, her nanny had bodily removed a girl from her playroom when she ripped all the electric lights out of Jenna's dollhouse. Later, she had lost contact with all her friends from college when she dropped out. And no one befriended anyone else in the syndicate. Jenna hadn't been able to rely on anyone else in her entire life.

When she met Erin, Jenna hadn't counted on her father ruining her life *again* and thought she'd have time to figure out how to be friends while keeping Erin at arm's length. She bought herself a couple seconds by drinking her coffee. How much of the truth could she tell her?

"Growing up in my parents' house was the worst. We always had to be 'on.' Dad didn't really care about what I wanted to do. I was supposed to study political science or law, get a degree, then either run for office myself or marry another politician's son and have lots of babies to boost his poll numbers." The shocked look on Erin's face told her she had her attention.

"Needless to say, that wasn't happening. I got my first tattoo at eighteen, then wore a bikini at the pool in full view of the paparazzi. I almost got disowned over that scandal." She took another sip.

"Which tattoo was that?"

"The popsicle." Jenna smirked. "But that was just the beginning."

"They had no idea what to do with you, huh?"

"No, they had plenty of ideas. They shipped me off to college out of state, and I was independent for the first time. But I didn't want to be there. I wasn't allowed to study what I wanted, so I didn't study at all. Instead, I partied. After a couple of years, the local media caught on that I was a governor's daughter and suddenly my drunk ass was plastered on every tabloid you can think of. My parents cut me off and quit paying for school, expecting me to come home with my tail between my legs. I was told I was going to rehab, and they were looking for boys who would 'accept' me as a wife if Daddy dearest did them some political favor."

"Oh, my God. I'm gonna be sick."

"Don't worry, I didn't go along with it. At all. I wasn't an addict, and I knew that. I earned my own way with odd jobs, eventually finding someone to help me disappear. Not that he did a very good job, apparently." She wanted to throttle him. She'd paid enough to make the new identity very convincing. "Look, I'm sorry for lying about my uncle. But I really do need to maintain the Amber identity outside of this apartment." She'd successfully run from her parents ten years before; it was the criminals she used to associate with that had sent her to Baltimore with a fake identity. But she couldn't say that to someone like Erin.

Erin scrubbed a hand over her eyes and sighed. "I don't like it. But I understand, and I would have gone along with it if you'd told me. However, I also get that you wouldn't have any reason to trust me right away." She smiled, but it didn't reach her eyes. "I've had to run once before myself."

"What do you mean?" What would sweet innocent Erin have to run from?

She waved her off. "That's a story for another day."

Jenna just nodded.

"So your real name is Jenna O'Malley, but you're working and living as Amber Smith because you didn't want your parents to find you? Yet they did anyway. So why not use your real name?"

That's exactly what Jenna couldn't explain. "Well, now there are death threats to consider, apparently." She snorted. "I'm not sure I buy that, but I'll use it until the election is over, and then I'll just explain to work why I had to do that."

"They'll probably fire you for lying on the paperwork. It's a contract."

She shrugged. "Then they fire me and I find another job." With another identity in another town. Damn her father.

"Thanks for telling me." Erin held her arms out for a hug, and Jenna gingerly obliged. She'd learned over their time together that Erin was a hugger, and she'd had more physical affection since moving to Baltimore than she'd probably had in her entire life. It was still weird.

"Are we good?"

"I guess so."

She squashed the pang of guilt when it rose in her throat. Erin thought she'd come clean, but there were things she didn't dare tell her about. She'd left a lot of details about her life out of that story, but it had all been true. Jenna didn't want to risk losing her only friend. She'd already had to cut the woman she knew only as Eraser X out of her life when she went on the run.

When she left to go back to her room, Roger was nowhere to be seen, but the bathroom door was open. She slipped into her bedroom to get dressed. After seeing him shirtless again, Jenna realized she needed some kind of armor to keep her libido in check. A sturdy, plain bra would have to do. No way she was going to try to seduce him with that old thing under her shirt.

"Hey, Amber? I mean, Jenna." Erin knocked on her door.

"What's up?"

"One of my coworkers is picking me up, so you can use the car again. I told them you were closing tonight, and I didn't want you trying to catch an Uber that late."

"Thanks a bunch. I appreciate this. I'll put gas in it this weekend."

Erin waved her off. "She owes me a favor, anyway. I know I'd feel better driving myself in this situation." Her eyes darted a glance back to the living room where Roger had slept. "Just wanted to let you know you didn't need to take the bus."

"She's not taking the bus until after the election's over," Roger called from the living area.

Jenna rolled her eyes, and Erin backed out of her way. "My father hired you. He didn't put you in charge."

"Hiring me put me in charge of your safety. That means yes, he did."

She growled and stalked over to the kitchen, only to stop short when she found Roger, fully dressed, scrambling eggs.

"I made enough for all of us."

"Thanks, Roger." Erin slid onto a stool at the breakfast bar. "What are you up to, Roomie? I have some grinding to do on my *League of Legends* character before work tonight."

Jenna needed a hobby. "I should probably do some laundry." Her uniform tee was clean, but the matching tank top needed washed — she got way better tips wearing that.

"How about you, Roger?" Jenna swore Erin batted her lashes at him, but after their discussion the morning after the LARP event, she wanted to think she was seeing things.

"I have some work to do before we leave. I won't disturb you." He turned around and set two plates of eggs and toast in front of them. "Couldn't find the jelly."

"I'll put it on the shopping list for next week." Those blonde curls bounced as Erin dug in. Jenna followed suit, suppressing a moan. These were super fluffy.

"What else can you cook?" she asked before thinking better of it.

"Not much. Eggs and grilling are the extent of my culinary skills."

Well, it was something anyway. He was a bachelor. He probably subsisted on protein shakes and takeout.

Erin and Roger chatted about LARP stuff, and Jenna felt left out. She scarfed down her breakfast, then rinsed her plate and put it in the dishwasher while they were still talking.

If Erin went after Roger, she wouldn't stop her. It was probably against his moral code to sleep with Jenna now that she was his assignment, anyway.

Sorting laundry gave her too much time to think. He'd mentioned the Army while he was talking to Erin, relating it to something that happened at an event. Roger was an American hero. Jenna was the opposite.

She'd fallen into the wrong crowd in her twenties, newly cut off and trying to make it on her own in a strange area. A homeless woman not far from her teens had been easy pickings for the syndicate. And once they figured out she could fit inside the ventilation shafts of the buildings they wanted to infiltrate, the money had flowed. She'd lived a little too well those first few years until her wake-up call came. On a job with one of the other burglars, they'd been followed. Her associate had shot the man dead without blinking.

Jenna had stood there in shock, her ski mask still in place. There was no way he'd have been able to identify them. But her coworker, who'd been with the syndicate longer than her, told her he was just taking care of a loose end. *"Our hacker changed the cameras, and he'd know. Then they could look for the footage and trace it back. Never leave a loose end."* She'd realized soon after that no one ever left the syndicate. Because if they did, they'd know too much. And loose ends had to be tied off.

After that, she'd kept her head down and worked strictly alone. By that point, she was stuck, not sure how to get out without meeting the same end as the security guard. He'd showed up on the news the next day, pictures of a family man who took his wife and kids to the theme park and volunteered at the local soup kitchen. The same soup kitchen she'd been at when she had been recruited into this life. And it scared the shit out of her.

What could a good man like Roger ever want with a criminal like her? Erin was a much better match. She did honest work, working as dispatch for the police and getting people the help they needed. Saving them from people like her former associates. From people like her.

Jenna shook her head to rid herself of the maudlin thoughts. She wasn't that person anymore. She might not have the most glamorous job, waiting tables, but it was good, honest work, and far less dangerous. It would be nice to talk to Eraser again, though. They'd had a good rapport, even though they'd never met face to face. She wondered if she was still at the same number, then immediately dropped the idea. Eraser might not tattle on her whereabouts, but she wouldn't put it past the syndicate to bug her phone, or even torture the information out of her if they found out.

Well, her laundry wasn't going to wash itself. Better get to it.

Chapter 8

ROGER SLID INTO THE passenger side of Erin's old sedan to accompany Jenna to work again. This was ridiculous. She had death threats against her, and she wouldn't even let him drive. It grated on his nerves to let her drive him around. He was the bodyguard; he was supposed to be in control. But he'd figured out during that conversation with her father that the only way to get her to agree to his presence was to give up part of that control.

He took advantage of the lack of music to bring something else up that had been on his mind. "What's the plan when Erin needs her car and you have to work?"

Jenna shrugged. "I usually take the bus."

"Public transit is not an option for you right now."

She bristled visibly. "I haven't seen these threats, you know. My dad could be blowing smoke up your ass and just hired you to prove he knew where I was."

And who she'd been living as, he thought to himself. But he knew that wasn't true.

"I have copies of the police report. They're legit." She snorted in disbelief. "Even if you don't care about your own safety, at least think of the other people on the bus. You'd be putting innocent lives at risk if you took it to work."

Her shoulders sank, the air out of her defiant attitude. "Fine. What do you suggest?" She sounded defeated.

"I have a truck, you know. I could have been driving you this whole time and Erin wouldn't need a ride."

She grumbled to herself. It would have been adorable if she hadn't been fighting him about this. "Alright."

"We really should stay at my place." His back wouldn't take many more nights on that couch. He'd have to see if his air mattress was still in his truck. More importantly, he had far better cameras and security monitoring there. He'd spent his morning setting up a small camera on the inside of her bedroom window facing outwards, and two outside the front door. He didn't want any blind spots.

Roger planned to add them to the app on his phone once he got settled at the Roadhouse.

They were heading down the highway when blue and red flashing lights startled him out of his thoughts. Jenna pulled over to the side to let the cop pass, but to Roger's surprise, the unmarked car slid in behind them. He stared. Those lights shouldn't be on an unmarked car. He knew the local police vehicles fairly well, and they never put such obvious lights on an undercover vehicle.

"What the hell?" Jenna muttered.

"You weren't speeding, were you?" He watched as a police officer exited the car behind them.

"No!"

The uniform was right, but it was ill-fitting. The hairs on the back of his neck stood straight up. Roger pulled out his phone and got the camera ready as Jenna rolled down the window.

"What seems to be the trouble, Officer?"

"Do you know how fast you were going?"

"I was going thirty-five, sir."

"That's not what I clocked you at. License and registration, please."

Roger snapped a picture and grabbed her hand when she went for her purse. "Since when does the Baltimore PD put those lights on an unmarked car?"

Jenna's eyes snapped to his.

The officer tilted his head at Roger. "And who might you be?"

"I'm Roger Hunt."

"Look —"

This guy was a fake. The police around here knew him from the incident with Nadia. "I own Hunt Security. I've worked with the Baltimore PD before." Roger glared at him. "I need your name and badge number."

The man turned three shades of red and stammered out, "I'll let you off with a warning." Then he bolted for the unmarked car. He drove off ahead of them, going way faster than Jenna had been.

"What the hell?"

"Fake cop. I got his picture. I'll send it to my contact at the police department."

Jenna gasped and leaned back against the seat. "Why the hell would a fake cop pull me over?"

"Why would someone threaten your father and his family?" Was she really that oblivious?

She stared at him. "You think it's related?"

Roger shrugged. "Could be. Maybe he's here to kidnap you and ransom you to your dad or make him change his platform for the election. Maybe he's just a random criminal that likes to impersonate cops. Either way, I need to alert my contact."

Jenna took some deep breaths, and Roger ignored what it did to her breasts. "You do that. Fuck, that's scary."

He turned to her, eyebrows raised. "Still think it's a good idea to go to work?"

"He's not going to stop me." Those blue eyes glared daggers at him.

Roger shrugged again, his opinions obviously unwanted. "Suit yourself."

He shot the email off to Detective Wells while Jenna got back on the road. Someday she was going to figure out he wasn't her enemy. Unfortunately, today did not look like that day.

The Urban Roadhouse was busy, even for a weekend. Jenna parked at the back of the lot, and Roger watched her enter the back door before strolling around to the front. He walked right up to the bar, where Cindy stood behind the computer, entering something for a customer.

"Hey, Cindy." He gave her a small smile to get her attention. Roger wasn't above using her attraction to him to do his job. "Can you tell me which one is going to be Amber's section?"

"Sure, honey. She's over there tonight." She pointed at a crowded section behind him with a bunch of frat boys. Lovely.

"I don't see any tables free."

"Yeah, that's Saturday for you." Cindy popped her gum and leaned over the bar. "You're welcome to hang here with me until something comes available."

He ignored her cleavage and knocked on the wooden bar top. "That'll work. I'll just grab a seat on the other side." He needed to see her in case of danger. That run in with the fake cop had his hackles up.

Roger placed an order for a steak and fries with the kitchen, then steeled himself for dealing with a flirtatious Cindy all night. However, not long after Jenna got on the floor, their boss and the owner took over tending bar and Cindy got her own section of tables. The dark, crowded restaurant made it difficult to keep eyes on his charge. Over the course of the night, Roger grew increasingly more and more agitated. There were too many people and too much noise. His fries got cold as he drew out his meal way too long, the owner giving him dirty looks the longer he stayed. Two days on the job and he was already causing problems.

A table in Jenna's section finally opened and Roger nodded to the owner as he took his plate over. Now he was closer, and the noise was even worse. He tried to get some emails answered, still waiting for a reply from Detective Wells.

He really needed to hire some people. For some reason, he had three different inquiries asking about his services just in the last twenty-four hours. Roger hated turning jobs down, especially if they needed help. But without a break from this assignment until the election, he didn't have a choice.

Not for the first time, Roger considered that the fake cop had something to do with the death threats. Forwarding the photo to Sam, he opened their text messages.

Roger: This fake-ass cop stopped my principal and claimed she was speeding when she wasn't. I'm worried it's related to the death threats. Can you see if you can find out who this is?

Sam: Sure man. It beats pounding my head against the wall on this Sly Fox case.

Roger: Still no sign of him?

Sam: Nothing. It's like he disappeared into thin air. His hacker friend must be fucking amazing.

Roger: Maybe he quit.

Sam: You don't quit an organized crime group. Not without ending up in a body bag.

Roger: Good point. Let me know if you find anything on Officer Dumbass, will you?

Sam: You got it. How does next month work for that vacation we talked about?

Roger: This job wraps up after the election, so as long as it's after that we'll be fine. Mi casa and all that, brother.

Sam: You're a lifesaver. Beer's on me when I'm in town.

Roger: I'm looking forward to it.

It didn't take long for Sam to come back with a hit.

Sam: My facial recognition software pinged your boy out in Nevada. A lot of hits in Vegas but also other areas, all in the Southwest. What the hell is he doing in your neck of the woods?

Roger: Fuck. Nothing good, I'm sure. I bet it's related to why her dad hired me. I'll have to call him and let him know.

Sam: I haven't found his ID just yet, but maybe we can figure out who's targeting him this way.

Roger: I owe you one. If there's any way I can help find your fox at all, let me know. And we'll talk about you coming for a visit next month.

His phone lit up with another email alert just as he overheard the table next to him talking to Jenna. They'd been flirting off and on all night with her, but this time, he couldn't tune it out.

"When do you get off work, Hot Stuff?"

His gaze flew to the table just in time to see one of the frat boys grab a handful of Jenna's ass before she could side-step him. Roger was in motion before he fully registered what he was doing, lifting the guy up by his collar and snarling.

"Roger! Put him down."

"Didn't your mama teach you to keep your hands to yourself?" he growled.

Frat boy had his hands in the air. "Hey, man! I didn't know she was taken!"

Someone tapped him on the shoulder. "There a problem here?" He turned to see some big bald bouncer in a tight black t-shirt crossing his arms over his chest.

"Yeah, there's a problem here. Why am I doing your job?"

The big man scowled at him. "Excuse me?"

"You're here for protection, right? Then why is she getting assaulted in plain view?"

"Listen, bud, you got a lot of nerve —"

"Alright, that's enough, you two." The owner, an older man with gray hair and a short beard, had come out from behind the bar to push them apart. He had a beer belly and no muscle mass to speak of, but out of respect for Jenna, Roger dropped the frat boy and backed up. "Amber, go cash out and go home. And next time you work, your boyfriend stays home."

"Now, listen, it's not what you —"

"Sure, Tony. It won't happen again." Jenna cut Roger off and glared at him.

The owner turned to the offending patron. "You, pay your tab and get out." Then he pointed at the bouncer. "Get back to the door and do what I pay you to do."

Roger pinched the bridge of his nose to stave off the headache coming. This whole thing had disaster written all over it.

"You. Boyfriend."

"I'm not her —"

"I don't really care. I am not letting you interfere in my business anymore, understand? You sit here all night, you don't even buy a beer."

"I *can't*."

"Don't come in here when she's working again, got it?"

"Look, it's not like that. I'm her —"

"Come on, Roger. Let's go." Jenna grabbed onto his arm and cut him off. "I'm really sorry, Tony." Her face was red as she dragged him toward the door, leading him out into the cool night air.

"You have *got* to explain to him what I'm actually doing here."

Jenna was silent until they reached the car. Then she spun on her heel and scowled up at him, wagging her finger somewhere near his chest.

"Look, you imbecile. This is my place of work, and I have to work here after the election. I can't do my job with you breathing down my neck and drawing attention to me!"

"And I can't do my job if you insist on acting like this isn't serious!"

"What the hell would any of my father's enemies have to gain by attacking me? Especially in public?"

"Who in that bar would stop them? The bouncer that looked the other way when you were assaulted?"

"And assaulting him right back was the right answer?" She crossed her arms and popped her hip out. "Guys get handsy in bars. I know how to shut them down if they go too far. But tips are better when you don't make a scene. You acting like a jealous boyfriend is the opposite of help."

Jealous boyfriend? That rang truer than he dared let on. Damn it, he couldn't afford to get attached to the person he was supposed to be guarding. Or maybe he already had?

He desperately needed to look at his finances and see about hiring another person. Maybe he could tempt one of his brothers away from the military. Unfortunately, he suspected that the election would be over by the time he could actually run the numbers.

Roger knew he had to put some distance between them. "You have got to come clean to your boss about why I'm really there. You *are* in danger." He pulled his phone out and waved it around. "I sent that fake cop's photo to my friend. His facial recognition software puts him in Vegas and other areas in the Southwest. What do you think he's doing here if it's not about the threats?"

Chapter 9

Jenna felt the blood drain from her face and a cold sweat break out over her skin. All night she'd fielded smirks from the other servers, women commenting on how hot Roger was, and how lucky she must be. She'd tried to explain he was just a friend, but it hadn't convinced them. And now, nothing would. God knew she couldn't tell any of them the truth! After hours of this, her last nerve had snapped at Roger's display of violence.

She'd nearly forgotten the fake cop that had pulled her over. The one who had attempted to get her license and registration. Without Roger's quick thinking, she'd have given him both her fake name and the car's address! And now to find out the guy was from *Vegas*?

Jenna's hands shook, and she heard Roger call her name as if from far away. Tires crunching on the gravel lot broke her from her stupor. When she blinked, she found his green orbs staring into hers.

"There you are." His voice was gentle. Roger led her to the passenger side of the car and opened the door for her. "Get in. I'll drive."

Shaken from the brief panic attack, Jenna didn't have the energy to argue. She did as she was told. He slid into the driver's seat and buckled them both, then plucked the key from her purse and started the engine.

Silence reigned on the drive home. About halfway there, Roger finally spoke. "Did it start to feel real?"

"Yeah," Jenna croaked. That wasn't the real reason she had freaked, but it's what she needed him to believe. Vegas was the syndicate's stronghold. She'd actually lived there when she was in the prime of her career with them. But it was also a tourist trap and a vacation hot spot. Hundreds of thousands of people lived there year-round. It could mean nothing.

She felt the panic leave her chest as she accepted that this was a fluke. But Roger apparently wasn't done.

"Look, when your boss has cooled off, you really need to tell him why I'm following you around. It's too dangerous for you to work without me nearby. I don't have anyone else I can assign to your case to help me watch the exits."

Jenna sighed and banged her head against the headrest. This was a nightmare.

"Why are you so worried about them finding out, anyway?"

She scrubbed her hand over her face, not caring about smudging her makeup to hell. "My life under my parents was ridiculously controlled. They insisted I go to college, study what they wanted, then come home and marry some politician's son to further my father's agenda. I was miserable."

"I thought that smile in your file looked fake."

She smirked sardonically. "They all are. Every last one. Until I got to college, and they left me to my own devices, outside of the classes that I didn't choose. I didn't want to go, so I didn't. I partied like a rock star. Eventually, the media discovered I was a governor's daughter, and before I knew it, they plastered photos of me drinking all over the tabloids. My parents read me the riot act for shaming the family. They cut me off, and I got kicked out of school. I was told to come home. They wanted me to attend rehab, and then they would find some politician's son who could put up with me."

Roger snorted. "Somehow, I don't think that happened."

"It didn't. I changed my phone number and learned to make my own way in the world." She curled her hands into fists. "I wasn't an addict, for Pete's sake. I just wanted to feel *normal* for once in my life."

"You were high on freedom, not the booze."

"Exactly." She turned her head to watch his profile as he drove. "You get it."

Roger shrugged. "College wasn't for me, either. I only went because my parents wanted me to. I picked the same school as my high school girlfriend."

He'd had a girlfriend?

"What happened?"

"9/11 happened." He took a deep breath and let it out slowly. She waited, wondering if he'd continue. "The university canceled classes, so I went back to my dorm and found all the guys watching the towers burn on the common room TV. One guy on my floor wigged out when they fell. We found out later he lost his dad in the attacks." He swallowed. "All I could think about was what if it had been my mom or dad? One of my brothers? Or my baby sister?" He swallowed hard. "And I decided I'd rather be sure those bastards never got the chance to hurt them."

Jenna remembered being in a private middle school classroom that day. Her parents had pulled her out of school, worried for her safety as a politician's daughter. Dad had only been a state legislator at the time. "What about your girlfriend?"

Roger stayed silent for a long moment. Long enough that she wasn't sure he'd answer. Then he parked down the street from her apartment and turned off the car. "She found someone else. Someone who was sticking around."

Neither one of them made a move to get out of the car. Jenna snorted. They had lived such different lives. "You know, until the day you showed up on our doorstep, I hadn't talked to my father since I asked him why my credit cards no longer worked."

He chuckled and shook his head.

She laughed to herself. "Yeah, I used to be one of *those* girls. But that was ten years ago. I'm a different person now." A true independent woman. Harder and jaded, sure, but she took pride in not needing anyone.

Roger gripped her shoulder. "You're hardworking, and clearly smart enough to dodge your dad this long. I haven't told him where you work nor sent in expense reports with the Urban Roadhouse on it. Even if you have to move when this is all over, you'll still have that."

Jenna swallowed the lump in her throat. How could this upright, all-American hero understand her this well? It wasn't fair. He might not do relationships anymore, but he deserved one. And in her mind, it seemed like only a matter of time before he found another one.

She hoped the woman he chose was worthy of him. Because it was never going to be her.

Roger unbuckled his seat belt and motioned for her to stay in the car. He opened the door slowly, taking his time to sweep the street for any signs of danger. For once, she appreciated the care he was putting into her safety. When he nodded and came around to the passenger side, she scrambled to get out. He locked the car and handed her back the keys. Then they strode side by side to her apartment door. At the bottom of the stairs, she looked up and noticed cameras drilled into the door frame.

"I don't remember those being there."

Roger shrugged and pulled out his phone, opening an app that showed the two of them on one of the cameras. "This way, I know if anyone's outside."

Jenna gave a resigned sigh. He should have asked first. "If Erin loses her security deposit, you're going to owe her."

"Trust me, once this is over, I'll make it so no one knows they were even there."

"Fine." She'd just have to trust him. And pray the landlord didn't make a surprise inspection. She hadn't been through one of those with this guy yet, but who knew?

The night was still young, and Erin wouldn't be home for hours. Jenna felt restless, and she wasn't interested in hiding in her room for another night.

"Let's watch some TV."

"Sure. What do you want to watch?"

"Gentleman's choice. I just want to zone out."

Roger snickered. "No one's called me a gentleman in a long time."

"Yeah? Well, don't get used to it." She suppressed a laugh. Roger picked up the remote and turned on the flat screen. He navigated through the various streaming services Erin had and landed on a true crime show. She should have guessed.

"Really? You watch true crime?"

"What's wrong with that?" he asked, taking the other seat on the two-seater sofa.

"It's just... True crime is for cops and old people."

"I'm neither one of those things."

"Oh really? You were old enough to enlist after 9/11."

"That only makes me forty-one. And I find it interesting. Especially when they talk about forensics and stuff."

"You mean how the perps get caught?"

He grinned. "Exactly."

She endured watching what these idiots did wrong to get caught. Most of the crimes were violent ones against women. It was practically a theme. Woman goes missing, no one can find her, then a body turns up. Sometimes, the cops immediately identified a suspect, while in others, they had no ideas. Some cases took longer to figure out than others. But every episode ended with the same conclusion: the bad guy leaves a trace of evidence behind, and eventually gets caught.

She shook her head every time they discovered a new piece of evidence. It gave her a new appreciation for how many idiots lived on this planet. After a couple of episodes, she forgot who was watching with her. "Why didn't he just use a lint roller on the carpet in the trunk?"

Roger gave her a funny look. "Well, they're lucky he didn't think of that or else the family wouldn't know what happened to their daughter."

Jenna bit the inside of her cheek. Granted, the guy absolutely deserved to get caught and rot in hell for what he'd done. But the sheer stupidity shocked her.

"What would you know about it, anyway?"

She squeezed her eyes shut. "Just common sense. He could have gotten away with it if he'd been more careful. All this show does is tell criminals how not to get caught."

"But I thought only cops and old people watched true crime shows."

And now her words bit her in the ass. "Old people could be criminals." And criminals could be a lot of people you'd never suspect. "And what about crooked cops?"

Roger shrugged. "They're usually cocky enough that they get sloppy, and then they get caught, too."

"Do you see a lot of them on these shows?"

"Sometimes. This one episode showed a serial arsonist firefighter. I think he got off on the power."

Jenna blinked. A person sworn to fight fires had set them instead? "That's insane."

"So was he." Roger leaned over when he spoke, and the nearness caused her heart to race. His warm breath over her ear made the little hairs on the back of her neck perk up.

She crossed her legs to hide the fact she was squirming, thinking about that night by the bonfire. Watching the dancers while Roger slipped his hand into her pants and stroked her to orgasm in the forest.

Her nipples hardened behind her bra, and she thanked past Jenna for putting on one of her sturdy foam-cup undergarments. Roger had turned back to the television. She thought he'd missed the signs of her arousal. Then one long arm snaked its way across the back of the couch. She glanced at him from the corner of her eye and found his gaze trained on her. Flutters erupted behind her sternum, and she swallowed the lump in her throat.

She had to get out of there. "I'm going to shower," she announced abruptly, then flung herself out of the couch and stalked toward her room to get a change of clothes. Roger must have followed her, because when she turned to head to the bathroom, his muscular form filled her doorway.

"What?"

"I apologize, Jenna. I didn't mean to make you uncomfortable." Sincerity shone in his face, both hands in his pockets.

Her heart pounded, but Jenna knew this man was not for her. "You don't do repeats."

He stayed silent, gazing at the floor in thought. "I haven't had this urge in a very long time."

"What urge?"

Another few seconds passed, the tension thick between them. Then Roger took his hands out of his pockets and raised his head once more. "It won't happen again." Then he spun on his heel and strode back to the living room.

Jenna hurried to the bathroom, locking the door behind her. She trusted Roger not to come in, but she needed to be alone with her thoughts. Looking in the mirror, she undressed without looking away from her own unflinching gaze. He'd told her what he saw in the car. A hard worker, someone smart. But in the mirror, all Jenna saw was a criminal on the run. Not from the law. She'd been too smart for them to catch onto her. But from the syndicate. Once this election was over, and Roger went on his way, she'd have to change her identity again. Maybe she could find a way out of the country, somewhere the syndicate had no allies.

She already knew she'd never forget this man. When the time came, she would wish him happiness from afar. Because once he found out who she used to be, and what she used to do, he'd never look at her the same again.

Chapter 10

Thankfully, Jenna was off Sunday, and she hadn't argued about accompanying him to his parents' house for Sunday dinner.

"They know I'm protecting you, but they don't know specifics. And they won't ask."

She'd nodded as she climbed into his truck. After his fuck up last night, Roger hadn't insisted on helping her in. But that meant he was left watching her scramble, inadvertently putting her ass in his face. Pushing the temptation to caress it aside, he shut her door once she settled in her seat. He walked around the hood of the Silverado and slid into the driver's side.

Jenna was quiet as they drove through Baltimore toward his parents' neighborhood. Radio filled the silence with his usual classic rock station. The house sat a little way outside the city on an acre of land. Pulling up the long driveway, he tried to see it through her eyes. Two stories high, with a wraparound porch and cheery yellow siding. Mom had been busy with the decorating, probably to make Finn's visit home special. Orange mums greeted them from the planters on either side of the door, and the wooden porch swing creaked in the breeze.

His brothers' trucks already lined the driveway, along with Caleb's motorcycle. He pulled in on the other side and parked the truck. Jenna looked like she'd seen a ghost.

"Don't look scared, Princess. They know the drill."

"Do they know my real name?"

He sighed. While he hated lying, he understood she had a part she played. "No."

"Can I be Amber here, too?"

"Sure. Fine." Roger opened the door and stepped out of the truck, shoving down the guilt as he watched her jump down. If she was sticking around, he'd have to order a freaking staircase for the truck.

Sticking around? Why would he think about that? This was a job, and a temporary one. There was no point in getting attached. He had already come too close to crossing the line last night. The last thing he needed to do was start thinking about her being around long term.

The only other time he'd thought someone was around for the long haul, he'd been sorely mistaken. Women couldn't handle a guy with a job like his. He'd never forget the day he graduated from basic training.

Mom had wrangled the schools into giving Jon and Finn a day off so they all could attend. It wasn't all that different from high school graduation. Just replace the hideous robes and hats with dress uniforms, and add in a lot more saluting.

After the ceremonies were over, Roger searched the crowd for his family and his girlfriend. The first one to hug him was unexpectedly short.

"Finn!"

"Hi, Roger." Finn, only nine years old, pulled back but stayed by his side, looking around the crowd of people with wide eyes.

"I missed you, buddy."

"Missed you, too."

The rest of his family caught up quickly.

"We're so proud of you, Roger." Mom had tears in her eyes as she hugged him. Jon pounded his fist and Dad shook his hand.

*Nadia stared at him from the stroller. "Hey, little sister."
He held his arms out for her.*

"She's getting too big to carry, Roger."

*"Not for me, she isn't." Nadia unbuckled her seat belt and
held her arms up. He lifted her to his shoulder, where she
played with the insignia on his lapel. Mom had put her in
a cute little patriotic dress and white shoes. "Let's go inside. I
hear there are cookies." Nadia still didn't look at him. "Do
you want a cookie, Nadia?"*

She nodded and finally looked at him.

*While they followed the crowd inside, Roger turned to his
mom again. "I guess Lacey couldn't make it?"*

*"I called her, like you asked. But she said she had a meet-
ing she couldn't get out of." Mom sighed. "I think they could
have made an exception, but by the time I got a hold of her,
it wasn't much notice. She said it was mandatory."*

*His heart cracked. "Did you tell her it was my last chance
to see her before I left?"*

"I did." She shrugged. "I'm really sorry, Roger."

*"It's not your fault. At least I had some notice. Even if it
wasn't enough."*

*Once he and Lacey married and she joined him on base,
this wouldn't happen.*

A small finger poked his cheek. "Cookie?"

Roger smiled at one of the two girls who had never let him down. "Yeah, sweetheart, we'll get you a cookie."

While they were in line for punch, Jon tugged at his sleeve. "Roger, we need to talk."

Good grief, puberty had hit hard while he'd been away. Jon's voice had dropped. "Sure, man. Let's get her settled."

Pouring Nadia a glass of punch only halfway full, they walked over to the table Mom and Dad had found with Finn. Roger sat Nadia in her own chair and left her with their parents. "I want to show Jon something. We'll be right back."

He found a quiet corner in the hallway by the bathrooms. Jon's face was serious. "What's up?"

"You know how I was mowing lawns and stuff?"

"Yeah."

"Well, Old Man Smith asked me to shovel his driveway and sidewalk this winter. So I've been over there a bit."

"Okay." Roger wasn't sure where this was going.

"You remember Marcus Moran?"

The name sounded familiar. Roger thought about it for a minute. "Wasn't he the quarterback for a while?"

"Yeah, graduated a year before you."

Roger furrowed his brows. "How do you know him, then?"

"He lives across the street from Old Man Smith."

"Okay..." What was Jon getting at?

His little brother sighed. "I'm really sorry about this." Then he pulled a piece of paper out of his pocket.

Roger unfolded it, and his stomach dropped. A blonde girl was kissing this Marcus guy in front of an unfamiliar house. The tote bag on her shoulder had pink Greek letters on it—Alpha Gamma.

No. This wasn't happening. Not his Lacey.

Roger shoved the photograph back at his brother, his breaths short. He wiped his clammy palms on his pants, but his eyes never left the picture. "I can't... I can't look at that anymore."

Jon tucked it away, his face full of pity. "I'm really, really sorry, Roger, but I couldn't let you go over there without telling you."

He swallowed around the lump in his throat. "I need a drink."

No. It wasn't fair to a civilian to subject them to his lifestyle. His ex had made that clear when he finally got a hold of her. She accused him of choosing the Army over her and reducing her to a side piece. He still needed to stay single. The business was his main squeeze now.

Jenna's eyes swept over his childhood home as they walked up to the door. Instead of knocking, Roger opened it and waltzed right through. Jenna followed, still looking like a cat in a dog kennel.

"We're here!"

"Come on in, Roger!" His mom exited the kitchen to meet them in the family room. "How have you been?" She leaned forward to kiss him on the cheek.

"I'm fine. Mom, this is Amber. Amber, my mom Judy Hunt."

"Pleased to meet you, dear."

"Thank you for having me, Mrs. Hunt."

"Oh, we're all adults here. Judy is fine." She waved Jenna's hand away and brought her in for a hug. Jenna blinked like she didn't know what to do with the affection.

"Did Finn get here yet?"

Judy stood, and he watched Jenna breathe a sigh of relief. "His plane got in last night. We have him for two whole weeks before the Marines want him back." She put on a brave smile, but he saw the worry in her eyes.

"He'll be fine."

Mom nodded and led them into the dining room. "Roger and Amber are here, so I'll lift dinner."

A chorus of "Hey" echoed through the dining room. Finn rose to greet him with a slap on the back. Roger returned it with a half-hearted noogie. Nadia jumped up from her place next to the dark-haired Caleb and hugged Roger tight. "I've missed you."

"Missed you too, baby sis." They were both busy as hell, but he needed to make time to see her and Caleb more. Although it sucked being the third wheel. He didn't know Caleb half as well as he'd like, and Nadia had moved in with him over the summer.

"Guys, this is Amber. Amber, this is my family. My dad, Irving." Dad waved from the head of the table. "Younger brother Jonathon." Jon gave her a flirty wink from his seat, and Roger scowled.

"I'm the sexy brother."

"Ew, gross, Jon." Nadia rolled her eyes. Roger shook his head. Jon was just being an ass.

"My youngest brother, Finley."

"Call me Finn." Finn reached across Roger to shake Jenna/Amber's hand.

"And this is my baby sister, Nadia, and her boyfriend Caleb."

Nadia rolled her eyes. "You should really stop calling me that."

"Nice to meet all of you." Jenna's voice floated in the air, and Roger wrinkled his brow as he turned to look at her. Where was the brash chick he'd been guarding?

They sat down at the two places left for them while Mom dished up the pot roast he'd smelled when they got close to the door. He piled his plate high with beef, carrots, and onions, then passed it on to Jenna. No, he needed to think of her as Amber, or he would mess this up.

Roger hated he was lying to his family, even if it was only something minor. *Think of it like LARP names. She's playing a character. Sort of.* He sighed, watching her out of the corner of his eye as Caleb talked about a motorcycle he'd been working on. Finn mentioned thinking about buying one, which, of course, had Mom in knots. Never mind that the contract he had signed with the United States Marine Corps was far more dangerous. "Isn't one dangerous thing in your life enough?"

Nadia turned beet red, and Caleb glanced away.

"Mom!" Finn barked. "Your daughter rode here on one. It's sitting in the driveway."

All eyes turned to Judy as she stammered, realizing how badly she'd insulted Caleb. But when Roger realized Jenna wasn't eating much, he was more concerned about that. She sat straight in her chair, far more prim and proper than any of them. She'd barely taken any beef and was nibbling at her food with tiny cuts of her knife.

He furrowed his brow. He'd seen her scarf down a burger just last night, so he knew she wasn't a vegetarian. He leaned over and whispered in her ear, "Everything okay?"

Startled, her blue eyes snapped to his. "It's delicious."

"You barely have any food on there. Aren't you hungry?"

She dabbed at an invisible drop of juice on her lip. "I'm fine."

"Little Amazon," he growled, "I've seen you demolish a pizza with Erin. That can't be enough food."

Her cheeks turned pink, her freckles glowing. "I didn't want to be rude," she hissed.

What the hell kind of charm school nonsense was this? "In my family, it's rude not to eat the food." He nodded at the healthy serving left on the serving platter. "I guarantee you Mom's got twice as much back in the kitchen as she started with. Why don't you finish it off, then she can bring more out?"

She blinked at him and bit her lip. Roger decided to take matters into his own hands when she hesitated. "Hey, Jon, pass the roast, would you?"

"Sure. Catch!" He faked throwing the plate, which earned him one of Mom's glares. None of them were actually that stupid, but the joke seemed to make Jenna relax. There were no politicians to appease, no one to impress.

He scooped up what roast was left and plopped it down onto Jenna's plate. Her cheeks turned pinker.

"I'll go fill it back up, Roger." His mom smiled and took the plate from his hand, probably glad for the reprieve from her motorcycle faux pas. "Save room for dessert! I made chocolate pie!"

"I love you, Mom!" Finn called out, a rare grin on his face. That was his favorite.

Roger chuckled. "She's spoiling you."

"She's allowed." He winked. "I seem to recall when you came back from deployment the first time, she made all *your* favorites."

"Ancient history." Roger waved him off. They all tucked back into their food as Judy returned with more roast.

After everyone sat around groaning that they were stuffed, Dad looked over at Caleb as he rose from the table. "Why don't I get the fire pit going? We can chat for a bit before pie." Roger furrowed his brow. Caleb's chest rose as though he was practicing deep breathing exercises. What could the kid have to be nervous about? He'd been with Nadia for about a year now.

Turning to Jenna, he spoke low in her ear. "Will you be okay hanging with my sister and my mom for a bit? Dad wanted to spend some time with his boys while Finn was home." He preened a bit when he saw she'd eaten nearly the entire plate of food.

She nodded, a shy smile on her lips. "They seem nice."

"Nad and Caleb LARP with us, so you can talk to her about that."

"Okay. Cool."

He kissed his mother on the cheek as he passed through the kitchen to the backyard. "Go easy on Amber, okay? She didn't sign up for this."

"I know you're not dating. Although she seems like a very nice girl." He knew that look. Judy Hunt had been on him to settle down for years, on and off. Once he turned forty, he thought she'd given up for good.

"Mom. She's an assignment. That's a huge line in the sand."

"She won't be an assignment forever." Mom dried her hands on the towel hanging from the oven handle. "Just think about it."

He shook his head and smiled. The Hunt siblings never doubted where they got their stubborn tendencies.

Out in the backyard, around a hundred feet from the house, Roger eased into his usual camp chair, the crackle of the fire the only sound. The Hunt men were quiet, which meant Nadia's boyfriend fit right in.

The younger man had his elbows on his knees, a can of soda in his hand. Roger shook his head at the beer Finn offered. Several minutes went by as the sky started to darken into twilight.

"Now, Caleb, why did you want to talk to us?" Dad asked.

Roger's head snapped to look at him. "I thought *you* wanted to talk to us."

Irving Hunt just shrugged. "I'm not saying I don't, but Caleb specifically said he wanted to talk to just us men while Finn's in town."

The man in question pushed his black hair out of his eyes with just the slightest shake in his hand. "I wanted to let y'all know I plan to ask Nadia to marry me."

It was a good thing they were all sitting down. Around the fire, three sets of eyes bulged out at Caleb. Only his father sat there calmly, a serene smile on his face.

Jon was the first to speak. "You're *telling* us? I thought you'd be asking permission."

Caleb snickered. "You know as well as I do that if I asked her father for permission, she'd castrate me with a rusty spoon."

Roger snorted. "He's not wrong."

"Anyway, in the interest of fairness, I wanted to give you guys a heads up. Especially with you shipping out, Finn."

His youngest brother nodded solemnly, a dazed look in his eyes.

Roger glanced back at Caleb. After getting to know him over the last year or so, he couldn't think of a better man for his sister. "Is there a ring yet?"

"I'm making payments." Caleb grinned. "Then I just need to figure out the best way to ask her."

Roger rubbed a hand over his jaw. "What about during a gaming session?"

Caleb's entire face lit up. "Roger, you're a genius! Then the entire squad is there for it." He took a sip of his drink and stared into the fire. "But how to work it into the campaign… she keeps her plans completely secret so I don't know how this would tie in."

"I taught her how to run a campaign. Let me feel her out and see if I can get some insight for you."

Caleb nodded, his face thoughtful. "Try to limit the spoilers, okay?"

"Dungeon Master's honor."

The younger man smirked. "There's honor among Dungeon Masters?"

And *there* was the smart ass his sister had fallen for. "You shouldn't talk about your girlfriend that way."

"Fair point." Caleb lifted his beverage to Roger. "Speaking of… looks like dessert is coming to us."

Chapter 11

Dinner at the Hunt family home was... interesting. Jenna was an only child of only children. Her main exposure to large family life had been through television and movies. Half of them showed a completely dysfunctional group of people, and the other half portrayed them as sugary sweet. Neither extreme made her think, "I want that." She'd been a loner all her life, and she liked it that way. But seeing the Hunts' obvious closeness opened her eyes to what she had been missing.

And after the cold impersonal mansion she'd grown up in, flawlessly designed without so much as a dust particle out of place, this house was a feast for her eyes. A patchwork of framed photographs adorned the walls of every room, capturing moments of joy, love, and adventure. From family vacations to birthdays and holidays, each snapshot told a story and evoked a sense of nostalgia. Trinkets and knickknacks of all shapes and sizes lined the shelves, each with its own tale to tell. Colorful seashells from a beach trip, souvenirs from faraway lands, and handmade crafts from children long grown up all mingled together. The air filled with a comforting mix of scents—the aroma of freshly brewed coffee, the faint hint of vanilla from scented candles, and the subtle whiff of old books. Every nook and cranny held treasures and memories, creating a warm and inviting atmosphere that enveloped anyone who stepped inside. It was a home that embraced imperfection, celebrating the beauty found in the randomness and lived-in nature of everyday life.

She'd wandered through while on her way back from the powder room and lost herself looking through the memories on display in the living room. That's where Nadia found her.

"Amber?"

Her head snapped at her fake name. "Hi, Nadia."

She had to crane her neck up to see the younger woman. Why was everyone in this family so damn tall?

"I overheard Roger mention you were at a LARP?"

"Yeah, my roommate is a member of Themiscyra. I actually met your brother at the event she took me to, because they assigned his team and ours to fight together."

"Really? He didn't say anything."

Jenna shrugged. "I get the feeling your brother doesn't talk much."

"Ain't that the truth?" Nadia adjusted her black glasses. "Did you enjoy it?"

Not nearly as much as the after-party. "It was... interesting."

Nadia laughed. "It's not for everyone. Don't feel bad."

"The party was better." She fought to keep the blush from rising.

The other woman waggled her chestnut-colored brows at her. "Was your tent rocking?"

"Don't know, I slept in someone else's." They erupted into giggles and Jenna felt like Nadia could be an actual friend, just as long as she didn't admit *whose* tent she spent the night in. Too bad she wouldn't be around after the election. It wouldn't be fair to put Roger's family in danger.

"Nadia? Can you come help me carry these plates out to the fire pit?" Judy's voice snapped Jenna out of her thoughts.

"Sure, Mom!"

She followed Roger's sister into the kitchen. "Can I help, Judy?"

"Oh, aren't you sweet? Sure, grab that tray table." She nodded at a folding TV tray on a stand in the corner. "We use them for all kinds of things besides eating in front of the television."

Jenna smiled. How wholesome and homey. Such furniture never would have graced her childhood home. Hoisting the blonde wood under her arm, she followed Nadia, who carried the plates and forks, and Judy carrying the scrumptious-looking chocolate meringue pie.

Judy had cooked their meal *and* their dessert. When had Jenna ever seen her mother lift a finger in the kitchen? That's what she hired a cook for. If she had sweets in the house, they were only for one of her fancy gatherings. And they were always tiny bite-sized pastries sourced from a high-end bakery that guests could eat while they schmoozed each other in the ballroom with marble floors.

God, she'd hated those parties. Her mother insisted on her presence, even when she was young and had nothing to say. The poor nanny would have to chase her around and attempt to keep her occupied. Once she was a teenager, she hadn't needed a minder, but she'd argued with her parents more than once about how she would disappear during the event. As an adult, she only had to deal with the parties during her breaks from college. Then it wasn't an issue at all.

Judy had welcomed her with open arms, while Eleanor O'Malley would never let a stranger through the door unless they had something to offer her. And all Jenna had offered here were lies. She closed her eyes against the guilt and remembered she was using that name for a reason.

Night had fallen while they were inside the house. The distant chirping of crickets and the hooting of an owl echoed through the stillness, creating a serene yet eerie atmosphere. The scent of the wood smoke drifted through the air, contrasting with the chill of the air. Judy nodded at Jenna to set up the tray table behind the men at the fire pit, then laid the pie down. Cutting it into eight thick slices, they passed plates and forks around the chairs. Nadia disappeared, then reappeared from some shed with three more folding chairs.

"Didn't think we'd let you sit out here without us, did you?" Judy winked at her husband.

"Just needed to talk about some things, love." He exchanged a kiss for his pie plate.

Ignoring the sudden heaviness in her chest, Jenna sat down in the chair between Roger and Jon, her plate in her hand. She'd never seen such an easy affection between her parents. Often she'd wondered growing up if they loved each other at all. That had been part of the reason she'd eschewed their efforts to convince her to go into a political marriage. It had been pretty obvious that's all theirs was, and she didn't want anything to do with it.

She'd thought displays like this were only in movies.

Once the ladies were all seated, everyone dug in. The chocolate filling was like silk on her tongue, the richness tempered with the meringue perfectly, all encased in a buttery crust. "Mmm! Judy, this is the best pie I've ever eaten!"

Chuckles rose around the fire pit, a warm glow on everyone's face that matched the one in her soul. "Thank you, Amber."

Jenna nearly choked on her next bite as the cold knife of guilt dug its way further into her gut. *You're undercover,* she reminded herself. *You're protecting yourself.*

"You can see why it's my favorite." Finn grinned at her from across the circle. He was handsome as hell, but there was no spark there for her. Even though he was leaving, and would be perfect for some short-term fun, it would be way too awkward with his brother around.

Besides, the chemistry that she'd felt back at the LARP event with Roger hadn't faded. He had a rugged command that captivated her.

"Hey, Roger," Nadia called out. "Why didn't you tell us Amber was an Amazon?"

Jon and Finn looked at her, confused. Jenna squirmed in her seat. "Technically, it was a onetime thing with my roommate. I didn't join as a full member."

Roger just shrugged. "You didn't ask."

Nadia rolled her eyes. "Why were they fighting with Melberth? We don't usually get pitted against them."

"It was supposed to storm, and they had everyone double up. We were allies, not enemies. And we kicked ass."

"Roger! Language!"

"Sorry, Mom."

"Wish we could've been there," Caleb interjected between bites of pie.

Jenna cocked her head. "Oh, right. Roger mentioned you play, too."

He grinned. "Corvon Silvercloak."

Nadia raised her hand. "Asteria."

Finn waved. "Brander."

Jon leaned over and purred in her ear. "Heimar."

Roger's arm behind her chair surprised her as he whacked Jon across the head. "Knock it off."

"What?" He offered his brother an innocent look, but then he winked at Jenna.

"She's my client, you — jerk." Roger glanced at his mother. He probably didn't want to get in trouble for his language again. Jenna snickered at the thought.

Jon leaned over again when Roger went back to his pie. "Can I get your number for after you ditch this wet blanket, sweetheart?"

Her spine stiffened, and she stammered as her throat closed around her pie. Jon was also objectively handsome, but smooth, suave men were not her thing. That's why she didn't appreciate her parents trying to set her up with one of her father's colleagues' sons. She'd never trusted them.

Roger rumbled at his brother, but it sounded more like a growl than words. "Is Annapolis not providing you with enough entertainment?"

"You know I like to keep my options open, brother."

"Jonathon Arnold! Leave the poor girl alone." Judy glared at him.

"My apologies, Amber." At least he looked contrite. Jenna hoped with the shadows from the flames, no one could see her blush.

She listened to the family chat around the fire, Nadia and Judy carrying most of the conversation. Watching the flames nearly put her into a hypnotic trance. What would her life have been like if her family had been close, like this one? Would she have turned out better? Made better choices?

Her thoughts wandered further. The two couples around the fire were easy with their affection in a way she'd never witnessed before. Her parents, if they held any affection for each other, kept it behind closed doors. And in the syndicate, couples had been rare. More often than not, they couldn't trust the other not to stab them in the back. There'd also been a rumor that circulated every so often among the low-rung members that the syndicate had someone's significant other, or mother, or brother, brutally beaten as a warning for some failure on the colleague's part. So if any of them cared about someone, they stayed the fuck away. Any emotional connection was a weakness that could be exploited.

Seeing Judy and Nadia curled under the arms of their men was weird. Like she'd stepped into a movie or something. Had Roger been like that with his ex before the military? Would he bring someone home someday?

The image of Roger with some nameless, faceless woman in her head made her stomach clench. He'd laugh at something she said, his arm around her as they made s'mores around the fire pit. Jenna shook her head to break the flames' spell. It did her no good to get jealous of someone who didn't exist, especially when she could lay no claim to Roger. Once this election was over, she might have to leave Baltimore. The whole point of coming here was to start over with a new identity and he'd blown it out of the water after only a few weeks, thanks to her father. She was back to square one.

Worse, she was stuck at square one with people who knew who she was but didn't know about her enemies. Roger had no idea what kind of trouble he'd saddled himself with, all for a paycheck. She scratched at her skin, wondering briefly if she'd been bitten by a late mosquito. Her mouth had gone dry, and she wasn't sure where the boys were keeping the drinks out here.

Before she could ask for a beverage, everyone was rising, talking about calling it a night. Nadia made a joke with Finn about sleeping in his old bedroom, although apparently Jon was also staying since he'd been drinking. Nadia hugged everyone around the circle, even engulfing Jenna. "Tell my brother to give you my number, okay? We can keep in touch even after you're done with this Neanderthal."

That broke Jenna's melancholy, and she laughed. "He actually lets you call him that? It's perfect!"

Roger scowled at his little sister. "What makes you think I *let* her do anything?"

Nadia smirked at him and tossed her ponytail. "Damn straight. I'll see you around, Amber." She sauntered off toward Caleb, both zipping into leather jackets.

Jenna sighed, wishing things could be different. She liked Roger's family a lot. "Your sister is nice."

"Yeah, she turned out all right." A slow smile spread across his face.

Jenna turned and studied at him. "You say that like you raised her."

He shrugged and tossed his soda can in the recycling bin Judy had brought outside. "I was sixteen when she was born. I guess it feels like it sometimes."

Damn, that was quite the jump. "It's amazing you two get along at all."

"We spoiled her rotten." Roger smirked. "She was three when I went to college. The first time I came home for fall break, she wanted me to take her out of her car seat and wouldn't let me go when I tried to put her down for her nap. It was the longest I'd been away from home at that point, so I just let her sleep on me."

Jenna imagined a young adult Roger, so beloved by his baby sister, that she clung to him even in her sleep. Tears burned in her eyes. She'd never felt a love like that, her parents preferring to hire nannies until she was old enough for school.

"Honestly, it's a good thing she was such a willfully independent child, or you'd have been carrying her everywhere." When had Judy and Irving snuck up next to them? Jenna blinked her eyes dry.

"Drive safe, son." Irving patted him on the back as Judy hugged first her, then Roger.

"Have a good night," she told the Hunts.

They were silent while walking back to Roger's Silverado in the darkness. Warm light spilled from the windows of the house built on love. Jenna's heart ached, wishing she'd had that type of life growing up.

Her mouth moved without her brain's permission when they reached his truck. "Do you think your parents would adopt me?"

Roger snorted, then he laughed so hard he threw his head back. It was the first time she'd seen him laugh since that night at camp, and it transformed him entirely. There was the man she had been drawn to. She stared, uncertain for a moment whether he was laughing at her idea or actually amused. Wiping his eyes, he unlocked the truck. "I'm going to tell them you said that."

"What's so funny?" Jenna ducked her head as he unlocked the truck.

"I think my mom would steal you in a heartbeat."

"Oh." Definitely the second one, then. "I wouldn't actually suggest that. I realize that would be awkward for you."

"Why? Because we've slept together?"

"Well, that, too." She bit her lip as he opened her door for her. Then, as she climbed into the truck, she suddenly became aware that her ass was pretty much in his face. "You need a fucking stepladder for this truck," she huffed, her face beet red when she'd righted herself.

"I don't usually have passengers." He smirked. "If you need help, all you have to do is ask."

She scoffed. "And give you an excuse to put your hands on my ass again?"

He leaned into the cab and spoke low in her ear. "I heard no complaints last time." A shiver raced down her spine. Then he shut her door and walked around the truck to the driver's side.

"Can I turn the heat on? I'm cold."

He nodded as he backed the truck up and took them back out to the street. But the heater did nothing for the goose bumps on her skin, because the memories of their one night together started playing on repeat in her head again.

Chapter 12

ROGER SAT ON THE love seat in Jenna and Erin's living room, all ready to accompany Jenna to her next shift at the Roadhouse. They wouldn't have to leave for a few minutes, which gave him time to fulfill his promise to his future brother-in-law. He dialed Nadia's number and lifted the phone to his ear. She picked up on the first ring. "Hey, big brother, what's up?"

"How are you, baby sis?" He grinned at the exasperated groan she made, seeing her eyes roll in his head.

"I'm doing fine. Working on the next section of this campaign that I'm running for the squad."

Aha. Caleb really did know when she was working on it. Score one for the boyfriend. "Oh yeah? Anything I can help with?"

She explained it had been a while since they all had time to game together, but now that most of her friends had moved out of the apartment building they all used to live in, they were making a concerted effort to do better. "And honestly, the last we left our characters, they were camping out after taking down a lich."

He scrubbed his chin. "It shouldn't be too hard to pick up again. It's not like you were in the middle of a battle or something."

"True. My problem is I don't know what else to throw at them."

"Tell me about the characters." He had to convince her to focus on Caleb's character to open up the opportunity for him to pop the question. Roger almost wished he could be there, but this would be more meaningful to Nadia.

Together, they worked out a story line where a rival would frame Caleb's bard for a crime. Then the party would have to clear his name.

"What should he be accused of?"

"Maybe the rival plants a stolen item on him. You know, like drugs, but some rich dude's things."

"Ooh, good plan." He could hear her scribbling down notes. "What should it be?"

He thought for a moment, then a brilliant idea came to him. It would line things up for Caleb perfectly. "How about a signet ring? The lord can't do his business without it, and it would be passed down from father to son, which makes it super important."

"Roger, you're a genius!" she squealed. "This is awesome."

"You know I'm always happy to help." He smiled, thinking of how Caleb could play this. Nadia was going to get the shock of her life.

"I have so many ideas!"

Just then, Jenna emerged from the hallway in her waitress's uniform. "I'm ready to go, Roger."

"Alright." He nodded. "Glad to hear it. Have fun, baby sis. I gotta go."

"Love your face!"

"Love you, too, Nadia."

He typed out a quick text to Caleb.

Caleb: Next week.

Roger: Your character is going to find an important ring planted on him. When he shows it off, that's your chance.

Caleb: You are my favorite future brother-in-law.

Roger: Just don't forget I know how to hide a body.

Caleb: Never.

AFTER HER LAST SHIFT, Jenna wore jeans for her next one. It was definitely no longer summer, and she didn't feel a need to make Roger sweat. Especially since he wasn't going to be in the restaurant.

That was going to be an argument and a half. She exited her bedroom, jacket and purse in hand. "I'm ready to go, Roger."

"Alright." He said goodbye to Nadia on the phone and pulled his own jacket on before turning to her. Luckily, he waited until they were in the truck before asking the big question. "Did you call your boss and explain the situation?"

"No, and I'm not going to." She clenched her fist and tucked it behind her leg to keep him from seeing how nervous she was. "You're waiting in the truck outside."

"Jenna!" He smacked his palm against the steering wheel. "I can't protect you from outside!"

"Tony will either throw you out or fire me. And then what will I do for rent?"

"Jenna ..." His voice trailed off and she could see the strain on his face. "You don't have to tell him everything. Just tell him your dad sent me to protect you from his enemies, and it's only for a couple more weeks."

"That makes my dad sound like the mob!" She groaned and slammed her head repeatedly against the headrest.

"He's going to think whatever he wants. The point is, I can't do my job from outside. We don't know who these guys are, and any of them could go into that restaurant and attack you. He doesn't need to know who you are, just that you're in danger. You're not risking your identity. I'll even show him my business license. That way, he knows I'm legit."

Her pulse pounded in her head, and Jenna tried in vain to massage it away. "I'll ask him to come outside with me and we can talk. But no promises."

"If you aren't back outside within five minutes, I'll come looking for you."

Jenna wanted to scream. This man, no, this *neanderthal*, to borrow Nadia's word, was going to drive her to drink.

Good thing she worked in a bar.

"I won't be responsible when Tony calls the cops on your ass."

"Then be outside in five. I'll park in the back. That way, he doesn't have to do this in the front of his establishment." Speaking of which, they were almost there.

This whole "fresh start" thing had turned into a nightmare.

"Fine." She stared out the window in silence for the rest of the trip.

When Roger parked the truck in the employee lot, Jenna unbuckled herself and jumped down from the truck. The gravel crunched under her shoes as she marched inside, heading straight for Tony's office.

The dark paneling had seen better days, the fluorescent lighting not doing anyone any favors. She knocked on the door. "Tony, can I talk to you for a sec?"

"Come on in," he called out. He was shuffling papers around when she opened the door. "What's up, Amber?"

"It's about Roger."

"Your boyfriend? He doesn't need to babysit you. You're working."

"It's not — oh, can you just come outside so he can explain things?" Her tongue tied as she attempted to explain who Roger actually was. Her stomach was in knots, thinking about revealing her identity. She questioned whether she could really trust Roger to not make things worse. "He's my bodyguard, and he said he can show you his business license."

"I don't care what your boyfriend does for a living."

"We're not dating!" she yelled, clutching her hair in both hands. "He's just my bodyguard. My dad hired him and gave me zero say in the matter."

"Bodyguard?" Tony looked as though he'd strained the muscle between his ears.

Jenna groaned, her voice filled with frustration and exhaustion. And she hadn't even started her shift yet! "Can you please just come out to the parking lot? Then he can prove it and I can get to work. Either he comes in when I do, or I can't work until after the trouble is over."

Tony sat at his desk, tapping his fingers. "He's not your boyfriend?"

"No. He's admittedly very attractive, but we *can't* date because my father hired him to be my bodyguard. And he is concerned about me working in a public place like this because someone could easily pose as a customer to attack me."

Why was this so hard to understand?

Tony rubbed his forehead. "I'll come outside."

"Thank you."

He followed her through the hallway, back out to the parking lot. Roger stood there leaning against his silver truck, rolling up the sleeves of his white dress shirt. He looked professional and sexy. What was it with men with fantastic forearms?

Ignoring the arm porn, Jenna officially introduced the men to each other. Roger shook Tony's hand.

"My apologies for not explaining my presence earlier. We didn't want to alarm the staff."

"I can understand why." Tony put his hands on his hips. It appeared he was still thinking. "But I'm going to have to explain myself if I go back on my words from Amber's last shift."

"I never told anyone he was my boyfriend, you all assumed." Damn her father for sticking his nose where it didn't belong. If he'd had to hire a PI to find her, then his enemies would have had to do the same. Frustration with her sperm donor and this entire situation oozed from her pores.

"I understand, sir, but we especially didn't want to alarm your customers, and this was the first chance we had to explain." Roger gave her a look that said she'd been part of the holdup as well.

Her boss eyed them skeptically. Apparently, the hamster wheel in his brain was finally starting to move. "How do I know my other employees and customers are safe with you here?"

Roger smoothly explained. "The threats were only made against Amber's family, and since her family is on the other side of the country, the threat is minimal. However, my client felt it was best to take precautions."

Tony scratched his head and huffed a breath. "Alright, come in through the back and we'll get you properly introduced to everyone." One of the other servers, Jenna couldn't remember her name, stepped out of her car just then. "Emma! Team meeting in the kitchen. Tell everyone to get there in five." With a nod, Emma disappeared into the Urban Roadhouse.

"Thank you, sir." Roger shook his hand and followed them inside.

"Amber, go punch in and meet us in the kitchen."

She was acutely aware of Roger's eyes on her back as she went into the main room to type in her code on the computer at the bar. The restaurant was almost empty, since it was the lull between lunch and dinner guests. Following her coworkers back into the kitchen, she stood next to Roger but couldn't meet anyone's eyes. She hated having to do this.

"Alright, everyone, listen up." Tony began. The chatter stopped. "Roger here explained he's not here to cause trouble. Amber's family hired him to protect her. I don't know specifics, but it's a temporary arrangement. So he's not banned, and you're to treat him like any other customer out on the floor. As far as anyone coming in knows, that's all he is."

"Hi folks. My name is Roger Hunt. I own Hunt Security, and I appreciate your help with this. The last thing I want to do is alert the people I'm watching for to our presence. We're hoping the trouble passes without incident and we can go back to normal."

The silence was deafening. Jenna felt every eye on her, wondering who she was. It made her skin crawl, but she held her chin high. Let them wonder. The truth was probably stranger than anything the rumor mill would churn out.

"Alright, that's all we had for you. Cindy, make sure Roger gets a table in Amber's section."

"Sure thing, boss." The blonde's voice dripped with what she probably thought was charm. Now Roger was fair game. Jenna groaned internally.

The night turned out to be a slow one, which forced Jenna to endure watching Cindy stick her boobs in Roger's face at every opportunity. After the third time, she walked away in a huff, meeting Jenna behind the bar where she was printing out a check for a patron.

"I know he's not your boyfriend, but he sure acts like it." Cindy lowered her voice in a terrible approximation of Roger's baritone. "I have to keep eyes on Amber at all times."

Jenna fought the urge to roll her eyes. "It's literally his job, Cindy. He's working. That's why all he drinks is water or soda." The check finished printing, and she tore it off the printer, ready to head back to her table.

"Does he ever take a break?"

She turned to look back at Cindy over her shoulder. "Nope. He's on twenty-four-seven. At least for a couple more weeks. Then it'll be over." And Roger would be out of her life. Although instead of things going back to "normal," she'd probably have to start over again. But she was exhausted and less committed to that idea now. The stress of the situation had to be getting to her.

"That sucks." Cindy snapped her gum.

Jenna shrugged. "I had no say in the matter." Then she walked away to drop off the check at her table.

On slow nights at the Urban Roadhouse, the atmosphere seemed to be engulfed in a heavy sense of stillness. The dimly lit bar was sparsely populated tonight, with only a few patrons scattered across the room, nursing their drinks in silence. The lack of hustle and bustle amplified her feelings of emptiness, making the hours drag on endlessly. As a server, Jenna thrived on the hustle, the lively conversations, and the vibrant energy that filled the air. Without that, she was left feeling drained and lethargic.

It also failed to distract her from Roger's stare.

When her last customer had just signed their check and her section stood empty, Tony came out of the office. He made a beeline for her as she stood next to the doorway to the hall.

"Go on home, Amber. There's only a few hours 'til closing. You and Roger can come through here."

She nodded. "Thanks, boss." Then she punched out, removed her name tag, and waved at her shadow.

Roger stood and strode to the bar. Emma cashed him out and then they walked in silence back through the employee hallway and entrance. She stopped long enough to grab her purse and jacket from her cubbyhole.

The truck seemed taller tonight. Jenna hauled herself up with the handle and sighed in relief. If the drive to her apartment was any longer, she'd almost certainly fall asleep. She looked forward to taking a long, hot shower and falling into her bed.

But pulling up to the apartment didn't give her the respite she craved. Roger made her wait when she went to put the key into the lock. That's when she noticed the door slightly ajar, and Jenna knew it couldn't be Erin. Upon closer inspection, the knob also bore the telltale scratches of a lock pick being used. Poorly.

"Shit."

Roger peered over her shoulder, his voice sharp. "Don't go in. Text Erin, let her know. I'll call my PD contact."

Jenna silently nodded, her heart sinking like a heavy stone in her chest. The weight of disappointment settled upon her shoulders, causing her body to feel heavy and burdened.

Her fingers flew on autopilot as she texted Erin, who was at work and could probably get a unit out here faster than calling the emergency line directly.

> Jenna: Our apartment's been broken into.

> Erin: Oh my God. Do NOT go inside.

> Jenna: We didn't. Can you send someone or do we have to call and wait in line?

> Erin: I got this. Stay with Roger.

> Jenna: :eye roll emoji: Like I have a choice.

As they waited in the chilly night air for the police to arrive, her mind whirled with questions. Someone had violated her sanctuary. Had anything been damaged? And who was behind this? Was it her enemies or her father's?

Was this what her victims had felt like when she'd been working for the syndicate?

The police showed up within minutes, bringing lights with them. They cleared the apartment, then dusted for prints. Roger swore when he pulled up the cameras on his phone. There had been nothing captured.

"Those bastards hacked my cameras!" he bellowed. God, the entire neighborhood would be awake now. Jenna pressed her fingers to her temples, feeling a headache coming on.

"How can you tell?"

"This fucking fly shows up starting at eleven p.m., goes through the same flight pattern about three times, and then the next thing you see is us." His face strained with so much rage, she thought for sure he'd throw something. Maybe his fists, or even his phone.

They were distracted when a man in a khaki trench coat strode down the steps. He nodded at Roger.

"Hunt."

"Wells." Roger shifted his clenched jaw. "They hacked my cameras. I got nothing."

"Email me the file. It'll at least give us a time to start checking the traffic cameras, see if they caught anything."

The two men bent their heads over Roger's phone. This must be Roger's contact at the police. He wasn't wearing a uniform. Was he a detective? As Jenna pondered, since Roger hadn't introduced them, Erin came flying down the stairs. "Amber! Are you okay?"

"I'm fine." She rubbed the back of her neck, uncomfortable with all the police officers present.

"How bad is it?"

"No idea. They haven't let me go in yet." Just then, another officer walked up to them.

"We're ready for you now, ladies. Don't touch anything yet. Just let us know if you notice anything missing." They nodded and Jenna braced herself for the worst.

Whoever broke in had ransacked their apartment. The couch cushions lay on the floor, and they had completely emptied the bookshelf of Erin's books. Drawers hung out of their cabinets and cabinet doors splayed open around their tiny kitchen. Even the dishwasher hadn't been left alone.

"What a mess," Erin moaned. They squeezed around everything that usually lived in the hall closet and went to check the rest of the apartment. Jenna gingerly peeked into her bedroom to see her things thrown about the room. Her bag. Where was her bag?

She breathed a sigh of relief when she looked inside the small door near the floor where a plumber could access the bathroom pipes. Whoever they were, they hadn't found her gear. Jenna replaced the panel and headed back to the living room.

Erin cried out from the bathroom. "Oh, my God! I... I'm going to be sick." She darted for the front door with her hand over her mouth.

What could have made her roommate run like *that*? Jenna crept toward the bathroom, praying this would tell them who did this. Was it the syndicate or her father's enemies?

Maybe the culprit had taken a dump in their toilet like one of those idiots in Roger's crime show.

But no, Jenna wasn't that lucky. Wide-eyed, she slammed her back against the wall, clenching her hands into fists even as her skin grew clammy.

One of Erin's lipsticks lay smashed on the counter. In the mirror, the words "Found you" stared back at her in hot pink letters.

Her heart raced as she gulped down air. Her trembling legs itched to run. But that didn't answer the most important question. *Who* had found her?

Was it the syndicate closing in to take her out? She'd be lucky if all they did was shoot her dead. More likely, they had more sinister plans for her. And anyone around her. Or was it her father's political enemies, probably planning to kidnap her and ransom her for whatever policy of his they opposed?

God *damn* it. They were no closer to answers than they were before. And whoever had been here was too close for anyone's comfort.

Fuck.

Chapter 13

ROGER CRUMPLED ONTO THE single armchair, the one piece of furniture the vandals hadn't been able to destroy. He ran his hands through his hair and tried to swallow past the lump in his throat. Someone had hacked his cameras. How could he keep recommending them to his clients when his own had been violated?

They had to get out of here. The top-rated security connections had meant nothing to these people, whoever they were. It wasn't safe, for him or for Jenna. They knew who she was with and that scared the shit out of him.

A stammering Erin came running out of the bathroom and flung herself out of the door, retching into the corner by the storm drain. Wells immediately kneeled beside her, holding her curls, and stroking her back. Standing, Roger's brows furrowed together as he crept close enough to hear her tell Wells what the mirror said.

"Found you" didn't give them a lot to go on, but it only confirmed what his gut was screaming at him. They had to go.

Jenna emerged from the bathroom, rubbing her hand over her forehead.

"Call the Roadhouse and leave Tony a message. Tell him what happened and that you're leaving town."

"But my shifts..." Her voice trailed off, eyes glassy and dazed.

"You're not safe in this city anymore." He leaned over and took her by the shoulders. "Pack a bag. We're getting out of here." When she turned around to go back inside, he looked up at Erin. "Do you have a place you can go?"

"M-my parents. I can't leave town. They're older and they rely on me..." Erin's voice trembled. She was a victim here, too, he reminded himself. Detective Wells placed a hand on her shoulder.

"You shouldn't be alone tonight, Erin."

Erin looked as dazed as Jenna. He raised an eyebrow at Wells. "Can you take her there?"

"Yeah, I got her." They communicated with a nod, and Roger followed Jenna into the apartment. Erin wasn't far behind him.

Dear God, the place was a disaster. "Is anything missing?"

"Not that I can tell. Honestly, I'd have to clean up to find out."

"And they won't let you do that until they've processed all the evidence." Wells entered the apartment after Erin.

With two big guys inside, this place was getting downright claustrophobic. Jenna disappeared into her room. Roger peeked his head in for the first time since he'd arrived.

She was shoving every piece of clothing into a duffel bag in a frantic daze. There wasn't much; apparently she could fit everything she owned into that black bag. She squeezed past him to go into the bathroom, returning with her toiletries. Those went into a smaller bag that fit into the duffel as well. Roger realized he needed to gather his own things, although he left the air mattress behind. He could get it later.

He tossed their bags in the back of his truck. This time, he lifted her into the seat. The fiery woman he'd been sparring with was nowhere to be found. After letting the officers know they were leaving town as a precaution, he started driving. To fill the silence, he explained his plan.

"We're going to a hotel tonight, then we're going to fly out of here. Do you think that ID of yours will get you on a plane?"

"It fucking better," she spoke quietly but with conviction.

"Okay. When we get to the hotel tonight, I'll figure out our destination."

She nodded silently.

He pulled into a hotel close to Baltimore-Washington International that boasted about its suites on the internet. The desk clerk handed over a key to a one-bedroom on the third floor that he assured Roger had a sleeper sofa in the living room. That would put him between Jenna and anyone trying to cause trouble.

By the time they got to the room, it was two in the morning, and they were both dead on their feet. But before he could let himself rest, Roger had to come up with a destination and see how soon they could get on a plane.

As he searched for flights on his phone, the shower turned on. He struggled to focus, imagining a naked, wet Jenna on the other side of the wall. Roger shook his head. Book travel now. Check on her later.

He secured two reservations on an afternoon flight to Florida right as the water shut off. Then he emailed the receipt to Governor O'Malley, explaining there had been an incident, and he was removing her from the area for her safety. Luckily, the airline didn't include the flight information on the receipts, preferring to send that in a separate email.

Rising from the couch to make up his bed, a wet Jenna greeted him in nothing but a towel, and he felt all the blood rush to his cock.

"Jenna?"

"I..."

The petite spitfire flung herself into his arms. She looked so lost, so helpless. Roger sucked in a breath and held out his arms, carefully turning his hips so she didn't get the wrong idea.

"I won't ask how you're doing."

She choked on a laugh. "I've never been so... violated." Her arms tightened around his ribs, and he stroked her shoulder. "I don't want to sleep alone."

"Little Amazon..." His voice strained. How could he both be a gentleman and *not* refuse her?

"Just hold me?" She pulled back, and he looked down into those crystal blue orbs and knew he'd do whatever she asked.

"No funny business." He forced the words from his throat after a much too long beat. "Let me shower. And you might want pajamas."

He'd be a gentleman, regardless. But it would be a lot easier to ignore his biological response to her if she wore clothes to bed.

She nodded and headed for the bedroom. He carried his bag into the bathroom with him, shutting the door and stripping down as fast as he could. The water was still warm when he flipped the knob, and he jumped in lightning quick.

Should he take the time to take the edge off now? Roger wasn't sure it would help, but he *had* to try before he resigned himself to sleeping with a hard dick. Wrapping a hand around his shaft, he recalled the feel of her in his arms, warm and damp from the shower. In his mind's eye, he tugged on the towel...

"I can make you forget, baby."

"Please, Roger."

The towel fell to the floor, exposing curves he hadn't seen in too damn long. Then her hands were unbuttoning his shirt as he whipped his belt off and unzipped his pants.

"I need you inside me now."

"I got you, baby." He didn't even bother getting undressed, just bent over and sucked on those plump, perky tits.

"Fuck me!"

He bent her over the bed and smacked her ass. "If that's what you want." Then he slid behind her and plunged right in, gripping her hips so hard he was going to leave marks. "Then take it."

He fucked her into the mattress, hard and fast, her cries muffled by the pillow.

In reality, Roger fucked his fist fast and furious, not coming out of his imaginary scenario until the evidence was washing down the drain. His cock had deflated, and the exhaustion hit him all at once. After a quick scrub down, he toweled off and checked the locks one more time before joining Jenna in the bedroom.

She had curled up on her side, facing away from him, on the side of the bed furthest from the door. He laid his sidearm on the nightstand where he could reach it easily, then locked the bedroom door and double checked the windows. They didn't even open, so they were good there. He was careful not to open the curtains too much in case someone was watching. Then, gathering his courage and willing his dick to behave, he slid into bed behind Jenna.

This wasn't so bad. He could survive this. Then she flipped over and pressed into him, and he felt the softness of those bra-free breasts pressed against his side. All he could do was throw an arm around her and hope his cock was too tired for more and would let him sleep.

Her breathing evened out almost immediately as she dropped off. His rest wouldn't come easily, but after this night of insanity, she needed it more.

Roger hated being on the defensive almost as much as he hated running away from a fight. Which was what he felt he was doing with this unseen enemy. However, it was better to retreat for now than lose the war.

Job or not, he couldn't imagine the world without the little Amazon asleep in his arms. Failure wasn't an option.

ROGER'S ALARM WENT OFF late in the morning, but he was already awake. At some point in the night, Jenna had rolled off him, and he'd been able to get some shut-eye. But old habits died hard, and he'd already worked out as best he could in the hotel room and showered again. He'd drunk half the hotel coffee but left enough for Jenna if she wanted any. He knew she wasn't a morning person, and last night had been rough. *Yep. She needs coffee,* he thought, as she stalked out of the bedroom, holding his phone and glowering at him.

"Turn. It. Off," she growled. Roger couldn't help his chuckle. It was so damn cute.

"Good morning, Princess. Coffee's in the pot."

She grunted an acknowledgment on the way to the bathroom.

"By the way, our flight leaves in three hours. I got us a late checkout, but we have to get out of here as soon as possible."

A sigh. "Fine." The door shut, the fan turned on, and when she exited she seemed more awake, her toiletry bag in hand. "Can we stop for breakfast? I'm starving."

"We can grab something on the way to the airport." He'd used his business account to get them pre-checked through the TSA, a necessity when you traveled with a firearm. It wouldn't be *on* him, obviously. It was going into his checked bag.

Jenna seemed back to normal after her scare, which made Roger feel better about sharing a bed with his client. Even with it being platonic, they had been crossing a line. But if it helped her settle, he was happy to do it.

Even if his cock wasn't happy with him when he woke up. Especially when she was walking around the hotel room in tiny little shorts and a tank top that only reminded him how her curves felt under his hands. He'd wanted to take her a second time that night in his tent, see her writhe underneath him as he drove her over the edge, but she had left before he woke up.

Shit. His dick was hardening, and they had to act professional now.

"Okay, where are we going?" Jenna asked from the bedroom. He heard the rustle of cloth and figured she was changing and packing up.

"I hope you like the beach."

She stuck her head out from behind the door. "In September? We'll freeze."

"Not in Florida, we won't."

"Good deal. I've always wanted to go there." She disappeared again.

"We're not going to Disney World."

"No shit," she said as she returned to the living room, dressed and carrying her bag on her shoulder. "Way too many people. I don't need these guys taking out innocent children in their haste to get to me."

Roger narrowed his eyes at her. She wasn't back to normal, not the normal he was used to, anyway. It looked more like she'd gone into some kind of survival mode, but not one he was familiar with. As in, she was taking the danger and risks into account a little too well for a civilian. Her eyes were as hard as steel as she discussed the enemy openly. How well did she know them?

"And too easy for them to hide in plain sight. No, we're heading to one of the beaches. I won't know until we get there which one. That will make it harder to be tracked from the airport."

She took a sip of her coffee, doctored only with sugar, since they didn't have milk in the room, and her face puckered. "Alright, well, I'm ready. Let's roll."

"We'll get you better coffee along with breakfast."

She nodded. Took another sip, then poured the rest down the sink. "Sounds like a plan."

Chapter 14

Breakfast turned out to be from a Starbucks with a drive-through. Roger wanted to get to the airport early enough to avoid any issues with security, which meant they didn't have time to stop. Jenna leaned back against the headrest in his truck, still exhausted. She'd slept better next to him than she had in weeks, but her harrowing ordeal had drained her beyond what one night's sleep could restore. And now, after months of living under her new identity in Baltimore, a time where she had relaxed and just lived her new life, her mask was back on. She hated it. But to deal with the syndicate, it was necessary.

It had to be them. No one else would bother pointing out that she'd run. After mulling it over, she'd realized that she'd grown soft and complacent. She had to get back to the person she had been back in Vegas. Hard, uncompromising. But with Roger around, that was easier said than done. He still thought he was in charge as her bodyguard. And Jenna had worked alone for a long time.

They left the truck in the airport's long-term parking lot, unsure when they'd be back. Duffel bags slung over their shoulders, they looked like quite the pair as they boarded the shuttle bus to take them to the terminal. It was empty this time of day. Most people likely left for their vacations earlier in the day so they could make the most of their time there, she supposed.

Silence reigned as she finished her latte, and they pulled into the terminal. Roger left the bus first, his eyes scanning for danger. Already her instincts had her doing the same.

But it wasn't danger they found. A homeless man with a tattered ball cap sat against the wall of the airport. A long, scraggly gray beard hung from his wrinkled, tan face. He wore his clothes in multiple layers, probably all he owned, and held a small cardboard sign next to a cup for change. Instead of heading straight for the door, Roger checked to be sure she was with him, and led her over to the man.

Jenna furrowed her brows, wondering what Roger was up to. He crouched down in front of the old man and stuck out his hand. "Hey, man. Specialist Hunt. Where'd you serve?"

"Gulf War, Sargent John Baruch." He named some division Jenna couldn't quite catch from where she stood.

Roger nodded. She observed their conversation, but she couldn't hear over the traffic noise. He was listening, nodding, and talking to someone she would have walked right past. Someone most people in this town would have walked past, if the dirty looks the other travelers gave them as they strode into the airport were any sign.

"Sir, you're blocking the sidewalk. I have to ask you to move along." A security guard appeared, but he only spoke to Roger. Not the man on the sidewalk.

Roger stood to his full height. Which meant he was looking down at the rent-a-cop. "Sorry, Officer. We're just catching up."

Again, here was the hero at work. He was claiming he knew this guy before, but in reality, they'd only just met. Protecting him from the officials who would undoubtedly like to get him in trouble for loitering. Her stomach clenched. Roger had honor and integrity while she was a criminal on the run.

This was why she couldn't get attached. He was so far out of her league, it wasn't funny.

Roger watched as the security officer walked away and then addressed his new friend. "Can I buy you a cup of coffee inside?"

The old guy shook his head as he accepted a hand up. "No, they already kicked me out once. But thanks. If you have any change, I can catch the bus out of here."

Jenna dug around in her bag for her purse, where she kept her bus pass. "Here." She held it out to him. "It's good for the rest of the week."

When he stammered and tried to hand it back to her, she refused, shaking her head. "We're leaving town, and we won't be back in time for me to use it."

"Well, if you're sure. Thank you, young lady." He clutched it close and blinked with watery eyes.

"Take care."

"You too, Hunt. God bless both of you."

And then he was on his way toward the MTA bus shelter at the end of the sidewalk. When they'd lost sight of him, Roger turned to her.

"That was a really nice thing you did." His gaze unsettled her. He was looking at her like she'd done something amazing.

Jenna shrugged. "Someone ought to get some use out of the thing. Maybe it'll get him to a shelter for the night."

Roger nodded. "I hope so. And now he can use whatever he had in that cup for food."

She walked side by side with him as they entered the airport. "How'd you recognize him as a soldier, anyway?"

"The hat." He casually shrugged, the sound of his nonchalant response barely audible amidst the bustling chatter. "It was only available to vets."

Jenna gazed up at Roger as they crossed the terminal, and her mind churned with a storm of self-doubt and insecurity. It was becoming a familiar battle, one that she had fought countless times before, but today, in the presence of this former soldier with his rigid posture and unwavering confidence, the war within her raged more fiercely than ever.

She watched as Roger spoke with the ticket clerk. His every movement marked by a control that hinted at his life spent in the military if you knew to look for it. The contrast between his controlled demeanor and her own turbulent past seemed painfully obvious to Jenna. Her fingers rubbed the scar on her thigh through her jeans, a constant reminder of the mistakes she couldn't erase.

She remembered the first time they met, the intensity in Roger's eyes as he helped her learn to spar. She couldn't shake the feeling that he could see through her façade, straight into the heart of her flaws. And that attraction she'd initially felt at the LARP kept trying to blossom into full-blown infatuation. She'd been fighting it at every turn, using her snarky attitude to push him away. What could he possibly find in someone with her checkered past?

He deserved someone better. Jenna felt it deep in her heart. The weight of her criminal history, the shadows of a decade spent on the wrong side of the law, pressed down on her shoulders like a heavy burden. Roger, with his clean slate and honorable service, deserved a partner who could stand proudly beside him without a trail of darkness in her wake.

He was a soldier, disciplined and devoted. Still serving his people with Hunt Security. And she was a criminal on the run, haunted by choices that she couldn't take back.

He'd fought for her freedom to steal, Jenna reflected, a bitter taste lingering in her mouth. Her mind replayed the countless nights she had spent on the wrong side of the law, the choices that led her down a path of darkness.

As they made their way to their gate, Jenna couldn't escape the persistent thought that trying to date him would be like a square peg trying to fit into a round hole in Roger's life. Her internal monologue became a chorus of self-criticism, telling her she was not good enough, that she would only tarnish the brightness that radiated from him.

With a heavy heart, Jenna excused herself to the bathroom, unable to shake the conviction that her past rendered her unworthy of someone like Roger. As she walked away, she couldn't help but wonder if it would be better to spare him the inevitable disappointment that would come from unraveling the layers of her complicated history.

Better that she disappear after his job was over, than he ever discover the truth.

ROGER WATCHED THE DOOR to the women's room as Jenna went inside. The terminal was mostly empty, but he still didn't like the idea of not being able to get to her if something happened.

Guarding her was more than just a job to him, though. He had to admit that now. Roger had never felt this protective over one of his assignments before. But now, Jenna's case felt personal. The money from her father was just a bonus. Maybe it was because they were spending all this time together. Maybe it was their history. After all, he'd never guarded someone he'd slept with, either. All

Roger knew for sure was that he would kill anyone who threatened the little Amazon.

Her gift of her bus pass to John had blown through his defensive walls. When he'd taken this job, he'd expected a spoiled little daddy's girl. Not the LARPer who'd given him the hottest night of his life, and definitely not a woman who would empathize with the homeless.

Although, since she'd opened up about finding her own way after her dad cut her funding, maybe she could relate better than he'd realized. She didn't talk about her past much at all. They both played their cards close to the chest.

That pass was going to change John's life for the better. He'd explained his sister had invited him to stay with her, but he hadn't managed to make it to her house on the other side of Baltimore yet. Her car had broken down while John was being treated in the VA hospital not far from the airport. If it hadn't been for their flight, Roger would have offered to drive him. But Jenna's gift let John maintain his independence and his pride. It was a far better offer than just giving the man a lift.

Jenna returned to the chair at his side as he thumbed through articles on his phone. "So, fun fact."

"Yes?" He looked up. She bit that plump pink lip, and he really wished it was him biting it instead.

"I've never flown commercial before."

"What do you mean?"

"My father always chartered private planes. And I stick with cars and buses, now. This is going to be a first for me."

He shrugged. Maybe he'd been mistaken about her. "Sorry, Princess. We didn't have that kind of time, or the budget." Daddy might have been able to charter it on short notice, but he'd have been calling the man in the middle of the night in New Mexico. This would have to do.

"Right, of course. Forget I said anything."

Roger went back to his reading, but his senses were still on alert. Apparently, Jenna's were, too. Her head darted back and forth anytime someone came close. Looking over her shoulder, looking over his shoulder, plucking at her shirt sleeve until he thought it would unravel. After twenty minutes of this behavior, he settled his hand down on hers, making her jump.

"What?"

"You look suspicious. Settle down."

That just made her start abusing her lip again.

"Seriously, Princess. Let me do my job."

She held up her hands. "Alright, fine." Jenna curled into her seat, flicking her raven hair behind her shoulders. "Your sister was right. You're a Neanderthal."

He tucked his phone back into his pocket and patted her shoulder. "You'll just have to fly with the commoners today, Princess."

Chapter 15

"You'll just have to fly with the commoners today, Princess."

To top it all off, he patted her shoulder like she was a *child*. What the hell? Where did he get off ignoring her valid worries about being recognized?

Obviously, someone had worked out who she was, and she wasn't talking about her father's political enemies. Although those guys would spell trouble as well, since they had gone so far as to make death threats. Her muscles tensed as she curled into her chair to make herself as small as possible. The stale air blowing on her neck from the air-conditioning vent made her nerves dance on end. The syndicate never let many members get to know each other. Hell, Eraser X and she had never met face to face and knew each other only by code names.

She briefly wondered what her former colleague was up to. Now that Jenna wasn't working for the syndicate, whose heists was Eraser working on? Had she hit any interesting system bugs lately?Fuck. Roger said someone had hacked his cameras. Could that have been her?

If it was, they'd be fucked. Eraser was the best.

But then she remembered anyone could be with the syndicate. They could be here right now, waiting to board the same plane. Then they'd be thousands of miles up in the air in a freaking sealed tin can with them!

Sitting ducks. They would be sitting ducks in a public aircraft, and she couldn't explain that to Roger.

Although, getting a weapon through security was next to impossible. As long as they didn't send anyone with hand-to-hand combat skills, they'd be fine. Plus, Roger had been in the Army. He could probably fight if it came to that.

Fighting had never been her strong suit. She'd learned quickly that she didn't have the stomach to kill someone. The syndicate had simply put her talents to other use; no reason to shed blood when it wasn't necessary, anyway.

A text message came through at the perfect time to distract her.

Erin: Hey, we have a problem.

Jenna: What else is new?

Erin: No, I mean another one. The police called the landlord who called me in a rage. He's pissed about the cameras.

Jenna: Damn it! I told Roger we needed permission.

Erin: If I don't take them down, he's threatening to evict me for breaking the lease.

Jenna: Shit. Do what you have to. Roger will just have to understand.

Maybe she'd tell him, maybe she wouldn't. If she had her way, she wouldn't be going back to that apartment, so it would be a moot point.

Without her permission, time flew by, and it was suddenly boarding time. Roger stood up. "Come on, they're calling our section."

She followed in a numb daze, her eyes sweeping the corners for danger, unwilling to draw attention to herself. Roger gave her the window seat, then took the one next to her. "Relax, Princess. The flight won't take long." She gripped the armrest, nearly jumping out of her skin when he patted her white knuckles. "Easy, there. What did the seat do to you?" Rolling her eyes, she crossed her arms and watched out the window.

The flight attendant went through the safety demonstration and walked down the aisle to make sure everyone had buckled in. That he flirted with Roger should have amused her, especially when the muscular man at her side squirmed just a bit. Obviously, she knew he was straight. But at least he was polite to the man who was just doing a job.

She latched onto the armrests again when the plane started to move. Roger, mistaking her surprise for fear, took her hand in his and started to stroke his thumb across her knuckles. "You have flown before, right?"

"Not in over a decade," she muttered. It felt too good to tell him to stop, and the gentle soothing motions were calming her anxiety. Let him think she was just afraid to fly. It was better than the truth.

She was terrified they had just sealed their doom.

The flight wasn't terribly long, but Roger didn't let go of her hand the whole time, even when the attendant came back around to deliver drinks and snacks. Once the plane landed and the seat belt sign came off, Jenna had calmed down enough to pass for normal. At least she hoped she had.

They swung by the baggage claim to grab their duffel bags, then Jenna dragged him into the first gift shop she saw.

"Seriously? We just got here."

She glared over her shoulder at him. "I'm Irish. We burn easily." With that, she dropped his hand and handed him a ball cap. Dropping her voice to a whisper, she said, "We need to hide."

"From the sun. Right." He put the hat on his head and looked in the mirror. Was there anything that man didn't look good wearing? Then he handed her a pair of super big sunglasses and pointed at the wide-brimmed sun hats. "That one might even cover your shoulders."

"Sold." She knew she looked ridiculous, but that wasn't the point.

They paid for their purchases and headed for the car-rental desk. The only thing they had with enough leg room for Roger was an SUV. Jenna hoped she'd be able to get into this easier than his truck.

She didn't question their destination until Roger had inspected the vehicle for bugs and they were outside of the airport's parking lot.

"Where are we going?"

"Well, I thought about staying here in Daytona Beach."

Jenna considered that option. "What if they tracked us through the air?"

"That's why I was thinking we should head north."

"North?"

"Yeah. Most people would assume we'd head further south. It will throw them off the trail for us to head north."

"Works for me." She kicked back and tried to let her muscles unwind. Her worries still had her on edge.

Roger turned on the radio and scanned until he found a station they could both agree on. He headed north on the A1A and they drove for a few hours, pulling off at a sign for Palm Coast.

"Let's find somewhere to eat. I'm starving."

"Sure." She didn't have much appetite, but she knew she had to eat to survive. And she was dying to stretch her legs.

They found a roadside diner next to a motel not far from the highway. Roger entered first, as usual, both scanning the restaurant for danger. The diner's façade boasted a classic chrome and glass design, with a prominent neon sign declaring its name: "Charlie's Diner." As the door swung open, a bell chimed, announcing their entrance.

Inside, the air was thick with the scent of sizzling bacon and freshly brewed coffee, creating a comforting symphony for the senses. The checkered floor, worn smooth by years of foot traffic, led the way to a row of cozy booths lining one side of the diner. Each booth bore red vinyl seats, the upholstery cracked and weathered from decades of use.

The counter, worn to a polished shine from years of elbows resting upon it, sat in front of a row of swiveling stools. Framed photographs hung on the walls, showcasing moments from the diner's long history. The lone server stood with a coffee carafe in her hand, chatting with an old man who had to be a regular.

She almost hated to sit down after being in that position so much that day. Her muscles needed to stretch, and the parking lot wasn't that big.

When the server told them to sit anywhere, Roger found them a booth in the back. He took the side facing the front of the diner, and then his feet appeared on the bench next to her.

"Ew! Keep those things on your side of the table." Jenna made a show of pinching her nose like they stank.

He laughed, a big, bellowing sound that echoed through the diner and brought a sense of liveliness to the place. "You sound just like my sister."

"Well, we can't all reach the other side of the table with our feet, Mr. Jolly Green Giant." She stretched her legs out as far as she could to show him. "See? I can stretch out *and* keep my feet on my side."

Something stroked her ankle, and she yelped at the tickle, jumping in her chair and banging her knee on the underside. Her squeal turned into a groan.

Roger grinned at her, those pearly white teeth on display.

She narrowed her eyes and glared at him. "You asshole. You did that on purpose!"

"I'm sorry you got hurt, Jen — Amber." He barely corrected himself in time. "I was just tickling you."

"When I have a giant bruise for the beach, it's your fault."

"I can kiss it and make it better when we get to the hotel." He said in a teasing voice, wagging his eyebrows up and down.

She could feel the heat from her face turning six different shades of red. Damn Irish complexion. "That won't be necessary."

Just then, the server arrived at their table. "What can I get you folks to drink?"

Jenna hadn't even looked at the menu yet. "Water, please."

"You want lemon?"

"Yes, thank you."

"How about for you, handsome?"

"I'll take water as well."

"I'll give you a few minutes to look over the menu." She waddled away, her graying braid swinging against her back.

Jenna spied the perfect lunch. "Ooh, steak salad." She placed her menu down and rested her chin on her hand, staring out the window as her mind went into planning mode once more.

If the syndicate found her, she could guarantee her life would be forfeited. No one walked away from them except in a body bag, and that was if they were lucky. She had to hope and pray to whatever god would listen that they wouldn't find her before the election was over; if Roger was with her, he'd be fair game in their eyes.

"Amber!" She shook her head as her attention snapped to Roger. The server was back, waiting expectantly for her order.

"Steak salad with Italian dressing, please. On the side."

"You want dinner rolls or garlic toast?"

"Rolls, thank you."

"You got it. I'll put these in for you."

Roger waited to speak until she was away from the table. "Where did you go?"

She squinted at him. "Nowhere. I'm right here."

He shook his head. "Physically, sure. But not in your mind." He tilted his head thoughtfully as he studied her. "What were you thinking about?"

Jenna's spine stiffened. "Nothing."

"Princess..." She snorted at that atrocious nickname and gave him a dirty look. Her eyes looked back out the window at the highway in the distance.

"Hey." A soft touch landed on her arm, and she looked back at him. He was leaning over the table now, his eyes soft with concern. "You can talk to me."

"I'm fine."

He leaned back in the booth, his eyes still trained on her. "I don't think you are, little Amazon. But if that's the way you want to play it, I'll play along." He waited a beat before continuing. "For now."

She crossed her arms over her stomach, where the table hid them, and looked out the window at the empty road again. This behavior was strange coming from him. It wasn't like they had a future together. They couldn't. Jenna knew she had no business dragging such an honorable man into her mess. He knew nothing about her past, and that's how it had to stay. If they were discovered, she'd have to find a way to make her enemies think he was nothing.

Roger could never be "nothing" to her, though. Their single night together would be forever ingrained in her memory to bring out on long, cold nights when she got lonely. She hadn't been interested in anyone since, knowing there was no way they could compare to him. And the longer this bodyguard gig went on, the harder it was to ignore their chemistry. It still burned wickedly hot, and she didn't know if it would ever die at this rate.

Although the ridiculous puppy dog eyes he was making across a table at her came close to dousing the flames. All because she wouldn't tell him what was wrong.

"Let me guess. You picked up that expression from Nadia when she was a baby."

He opened his mouth, then closed it again with an audible click of his teeth. "Food's here."

She looked down at the salad topped with steak strips grilled to perfection in front of her. "Thanks." Pouring her dressing on top, she ate without looking at him. The election was in two weeks. She had to put some distance between them emotionally, since physically it wasn't possible yet.

Chapter 16

Roger led Jenna into the first hotel he'd found online that had good reviews. A clerk sat behind the reception desk, their fingers typing away at a keyboard.

"Good evening. Can I help you?"

"Yes, we need rooms for the night."

They typed some more and clicked around with the mouse. "You're in luck. I have one king room left."

"One room left?"

"Yes, the convention in town has us booked solid this week."

"What floor is it on?"

"First floor."

Roger mulled it over for a moment. With some kind of convention in this odd Florida town, there wasn't any point trying a different hotel. He couldn't afford to be picky. There hadn't been any patios or balconies when they circled the building, which was the only thing that made it tolerable. He hoped Jenna didn't mind making it their home base for the foreseeable future.

"We'll take it. And a roll-away bed if you have one."

"I'm afraid all of our cots are spoken for, but I'll put you at the top of the list for the first one that comes available." They smiled politely. "How long will you be staying?"

Two weeks until the election. But a thought had occurred on the flight down. If he could get Sam to help catch these guys, then maybe they wouldn't need that long.

"Let's say a week, and can we put a note in there that we might need to extend our stay?"

"Sure, sir. I just need a name, an ID, and a card."

He handed over his license and his credit card, but spoke low, leaning over the desk. "I'd like the room unlisted, please."

They didn't even blink. "Not a problem, sir." That was a trick he'd picked up in some security training he took after he left the Army. It meant if someone called and asked for him or an Amber Smith, they would be told there was no one there by that name. It was a safety precaution often utilized by celebrities and abuse victims on the run.

The last thing he wanted was to put an entire hotel of people and staff in the crosshairs of these psychopaths.

The clerk typed some more, then printed out the receipt for Roger to sign, and handed back his cards. "Your room number is written right here. Enjoy your stay!"

"Thank you." He hoisted his bag back up on his shoulder and followed the signs toward their room, Jenna at his side.

She'd been quiet throughout their dinner, and she kept the hat and sunglasses on even inside the hotel. It made her look like a stuck-up trophy wife, but he understood why she did it. The clerk probably thought she was a celebrity of some kind, and to be fair, she basically was. Just maybe not in this part of the country.

The green patterned carpet absorbed the sound of their steps. Murmurs of televisions escaped a room or two. It was late; most guests were probably getting ready for bed now. Room 116 was at the end of the hallway. He noted the fire exit opened only one way, and it bore a sign indicating that the alarm would sound if someone opened the door. They had neighbors to the right and across the hall. No noise from either room, so either they were asleep, or they were still out somewhere.

The door snicked open at the slide of the key card, and Roger pushed through the door. Cold air from an air conditioning unit greeted him. Even in the fall, Florida was hot and humid.

He motioned for Jenna to stay next to the door while he swept the room as a precaution. There was no way anyone could have predicted this move from them, since he hadn't known where they were going until today. He even opened the microwave and the refrigerator, which would come in handy. Eating out all the time got old, fast.

"We're clear, Jenna." Still, she stood next to the heavy wooden door. "It's safe."

She mumbled something to herself and set her duffel bag on the luggage cart in the closet. Then she tore the hat and sunglasses off her head and set them on the entertainment stand above the microwave refrigerator combo.

"What?"

"Nothing." She turned on her heel and headed back to her bag. "I'm going to shower."

"Sounds good." He watched her with a wary eye as she gathered a change of clothes and slipped into the bathroom, shutting the door behind her. Soft sobs were quickly drowned out by running water, and he rubbed at the tightness in his chest. Pulling his laptop out of his bag, Roger set it on the desk in the corner and fired it up.

Last night, he'd texted Sam asking him to take a look at the cameras to see if he could trace the hacker who'd looped the footage and allowed these political activists or whoever they were into Jenna and Erin's apartment. He hadn't been able to log in to grant Sam the access he needed until now. It was a simple matter of encrypting a file with his login and password and dropping it through Discord.

Sam showed up as "Online" and sent him a thumbs up reaction to show he got the message. After sending him a thank you and the promise of more alcohol in return for the favor, Roger logged off. He turned the laptop off and stuffed it back in his bag just in time for a downcast Jenna to emerge from the bathroom, steam billowing out of the door.

He leaned his arms on the desk and studied her. "What's bothering you, little Amazon?"

She sat on the end of the bed, brushing her hair with her back to him. "Everything is ruined," came her answer.

Rising from the desk, he drew close enough to see her red, puffy eyes. He knew he'd heard her crying in the shower. A stabbing sensation in his chest halted his steps. "Jenna... sweetheart, what are you talking about?"

She lowered the brush and gazed through it to the floor. "Dad found me too easily. Who's saying *they* won't? And they have way more motivation than him." Her lower lip quivered. "So much for my fresh start."

Roger shook his head. "I know you and your dad don't see eye to eye on a lot of things, but I can tell you this: there is no one more motivated to find someone than a worried parent." He snorted. "Or brother, in my sister's case."

She shivered as she stared off into space. "Not like them."

He kneeled, so he was looking up at her, and she couldn't look away. "Can I tell you a story?" Roger waited patiently until she nodded. "Last year, Nadia and Caleb had a fight. An hour later, Caleb leaves to go find her, thinking she left, but her car was still at the shop below where he lives. He goes into the office, thinking maybe she's there, since she was helping his dad with the books. No Nadia, but there is a note on the computer telling Caleb to call off a theft investigation if he wants to see his girlfriend again."

The blue eyes that were focused on his face widened.

"The note said not to call the cops. Instead, Caleb called me." At that, he grinned. "I almost hung up on him. But all he had to say was 'Nadia's been taken,' and I was ready to go to war again." Her hand covered her mouth.

"We got lucky and were able to find her quickly. But nothing, and I mean *nothing*, would have stood between me, Finn, and our little sister." He leaned in closer, lowering his voice to just above a whisper. "If the devil himself had taken her to Hell, we would have gone in after her."

He was close enough to her face that he could watch as the tears welled up, and her lower lip trembled. Immediately he tried to calm her. "Hey, it's okay. We found her. My point was, your parents are way more motivated to find you than whoever is trying to use you to hurt your dad."

She sniffed, and a tear escaped from its cage. "That's not... you're just... you're so *good*!"

Roger shook his head, his brows furrowed in confusion. "Come again?"

Jenna lost the fight against her emotions. Tears streamed down her face as he focused on making out her words. "You're such a... good guy, and I'm ... such a ... a *mess*!" she sobbed. "I'm lying to my coworkers, to my boss. I lied to Erin for months, and I lied to you!" Her shoulders shook as she gasped for breath. "I can't go back to the apartment, but I have nowhere else to go. Nowhere is safe. I can't keep dragging innocent, *good* people into my chaos!"

One thing he couldn't abide was women's tears. They made him want to tear someone apart. Namely, whoever made said woman cry. But it sounded like she was crying because she felt like he was a... a better person than she was?

"Sweetheart, I'm not a good guy. Do you know how many terrible things I've done under the American flag? I wasn't just in the Army, I was a Green Beret. They paint those red stripes in blood."

She shook her head, wiping at her face. "T-that just makes you an American hero. You probably walk old ladies across the street."

He shook his head, daring to take her hands in his. "Can't say I ever have. I know how to kill a man about ten different ways, though."

Jenna rolled her eyes. "You only killed bad guys."

"Bad is in the eye of the beholder. Every villain is the hero in their own story." He thumbed some of the tears from her cheek. "I turned their wives into widows, and I bet they curse me for it."

"Or maybe they bless you for it. You don't know." She crossed her arms, a challenge in her eyes. Why was she determined to be right about *this*?

He shrugged. "That's between them and their god. To me, it was a job."

She choked as the tears started up again. "Like I'm a... a job."

Aw, shit. His heart was either breaking in two or growing three sizes. He wasn't sure which. Roger turned and slid up onto the bed in a fluid motion that had her gasping in surprise as he wrapped his arms around her.

"You are *not* just a job, Princess. I don't know how, but your cute little ass wormed your way under my skin, and I don't want this assignment to end. I feel guilty taking your father's money at all."

She sniffed, a smile fighting to peek through. "Don't give it back. He can afford it."

He chuckled. "Okay." He stroked her arm up and down, his shirt growing wet from Jenna burying her face in his chest. Gradually, her breathing slowed, and eventually her tears stopped. She pulled back, but he didn't let her go as she wiped her face with her hands.

"I'm sorry. I don't understand what got into me." She chuckled sardonically.

He kept stroking her arm. "You've had a rough forty-eight hours, little Amazon. These aren't easy things to deal with. You're allowed to fall apart."

She turned her tear-stained face up to him. "Will you... will you help put me back together?"

And he answered from his heart, "Always." Then he leaned down and kissed the saline from her lips.

Chapter 17

THIS WAS EXACTLY WHAT she needed. His lips were on hers, his fingers gliding through her hair to cup the back of her head, and his powerful arm wrapped around her waist. Her lips opened on a sigh, and his tongue dipped inside. When she reached for him, she heard the intake of his breath, and then that huge hand angled her head and deepened their kiss. She dug her nails into his back, and his tongue returned, more insistent, but still gentle.

Desire flared. Her breasts ached for his touch, but the way he held her felt too good. She drew her hands around his front and pushed them up his chest until she could loop them behind his neck.

She broke their kiss with a gasp, quickly taking a breath, then diving back in. His fingers tightened their hold on her head, his other hand pulling her shirt up in the back so he could feel her skin. A moan reverberated in her throat, and he pulled back. She whined at the loss, looking up at him from beneath hooded eyes.

That green gaze pierced hers. "I need words, little Amazon. Do you want this?"

"I need you. Please, Roger."

He nodded, then picked her up and walked around the bed, laying her down with her head on the pillows. First his shoes came off, and then he pulled his t-shirt over his head, and Jenna was treated to all that sun-kissed skin over his muscular abs and pecs. She sat up to pull her own off, but he grabbed her hands.

"Let me."

She nodded, her pussy clenching. Releasing her wrists, Roger stood back up and finished stripping as she watched. Gulping as his erection bobbed free, it seemed bigger than she remembered it. It didn't escape her notice that he'd stripped completely bare for her before expecting the same.

He straddled her legs on the bed, forcing her to lie back as his body came over hers. Those intense eyes filled her vision until he kissed her again, and her eyes closed in pleasure. She buried her fingers in his thick, chestnut hair and kissed him back with the fire that threatened to burn her alive.

Slowly, his hands crept up her sides, pulling her shirt with them. When his thumbs teased the sides of her breasts, she released him and lifted her arms, submitting. They only broke the kiss to get the fabric over her head. Then his lips were back on hers, and his hands were everywhere. Cupping her breasts, peeling her shorts off her hips and leaving them right above her knees. Firmly teasing her nipples until she writhed and moaned under him, effectively tied down and at his mercy. With a desperate whine, she tore her mouth from his. "Please, Roger."

He hummed, a small smile on his lips. "My Amazon begs so prettily." He circled her wrists with one hand and laid them gently above her head. "These stay here. Or I stop."

She nodded. Right now, she'd give him anything.

He started kissing down her neck and Jenna fisted the pillow at her head to give her hands something to do. And to keep him from stopping.

True to his word, Roger kept going as though her desperation was contagious. His mouth took his fill of her tits, sucking and licking and flicking that wicked tongue over her nipples. Rough hands gripped her shorts and shoved them off her legs, then pulled her underwear off and tossed them over his shoulder. Then, his pace gentled once more, and Jenna wanted to scream. A pathetic whimper built in her throat. Until his fingers danced between her legs and tested her readiness.

"Roger, please. I need you inside me. Don't tease me anymore."

One hand kept playing in her pussy while he sat up and used the other to pull a condom out of his jeans pocket. Watching him use his teeth to open the foil packet made her wetter. He only stopped to slide it over his dick. Then he opened her legs and placed the length of his cock against her opening. Not going inside, he just slid along her lips as he lifted her legs and crooked them over his elbows.

Her clit throbbed as the orgasm built in her core. She could feel her arousal growing and rubbed all that lubricant over his cock. A whine started up in her throat as she tried to shift her hips to get him where she needed him.

"Patience," he murmured.

"I'm so empty."

He popped her knees up onto his shoulders, lifted her ass with one hand and slid two fingers inside her channel with the other. Then, with one stroke to her g-spot, she detonated.

When she came back to Earth, he was slowly sliding his fingers back and forth, rolling his thumb slowly over her sensitized clit. "You're gonna choke my cock so good, aren't you, baby?"

Gasping for air, her arms had gone stiff above her head. "I want to touch you."

"Alright."

The word had no sooner left his lips than she'd dug her fingers back into his hair and was pulling him down for another kiss. This connection between them had started back at camp, but it had grown stronger with their reconnection in the real world. She told him how she felt with her tongue instead of words.

"I hope you're ready for me."

"Yesssss," she hissed as he slid home.

He paused, giving her a second to adjust to his girth. Then he began to thrust. This position made him go deeper than anyone had ever been. The whole time, his face hovered over hers, warm mossy eyes filled with more than desire or lust. It took her a moment to recognize that the look on his face matched the feeling in her chest. All the while, his slow, steady pace built up her orgasm layer by layer.

For her, sex had always been hurried and fast, a means to an end. No one had ever treated it, treated *her* like something to savor. Dear God, was he… He was *making love* to her.

Tears welled up in her eyes, and his rhythm faltered. "Don't stop," she whispered.

He shook his head. "Never."

Then he started moving faster, building her up higher and higher. Sweat beaded on his brow, and his biceps bulged next to her head. Their breaths mingled, and she dug her nails into his shoulders as her legs trembled.

"Come with me." She couldn't hold it off any longer.

He swallowed her scream, groaning into her mouth with his own release as a white-hot heat enveloped her entire body. She shook and shuddered through her climax, feeling herself fall apart. But there was Roger above her, holding her together.

Helping her glue all her pieces back where they belonged.

ROGER'S PHONE LIT UP with a notification somewhere around three in the morning. He'd become a light sleeper in the Army, which meant the blinking screen had him awake in a moment. A quick peek told him it was just a bank deposit notification. Governor O'Malley's payment had come through right on time.

And the governor's daughter was asleep on his chest.

Nausea turned his stomach as the guilt and shame racked his mind. Part of the problem with being a light sleeper was that once he was up, it took ages for him to get back to sleep. He thought about the rescue missions he'd completed as a soldier. If he'd slept with a charge, he'd have been at risk of being court-martialed. At the very least, he'd be on latrine duty for a month.

He heard his old commanding officer's voice in his head. *"Don't get attached. You'll compromise the mission."* But he wasn't in the Army any longer, and Jenna wasn't a potential safety risk.

Could this compromise *her* safety, though? Roger considered it as she slept on, unaware. He didn't see how. If anything, she'd be safer because she'd let him stay close.

She shifted in her sleep, and he ran his fingers through her dark hair until she settled back down with a sigh. This was the first time in a long time he'd had a woman stay in his bed the whole night. He'd worked hard to keep women at arm's length since his enlistment, having learned the hard way that civilian women couldn't handle his job. Jenna had changed all that. He didn't want to go back to his lonely existence anymore.

There were two barriers to their taking this beyond their end date. One, how would she feel about the dangers of his job, and the long hours it required? And two, her father.

Roger reminded himself Governor O'Malley was on the other side of the country and had only talked to his daughter once in the last ten years. Jenna clearly didn't give a damn about her parents' opinion, and he could respect that. She'd surprised him. When he got that call from New Mexico, he expected to find a stuck-up society princess, not his little Amazon warrior. If it hadn't been for the short-as-hell dress in that old photo showing off her tasty tattoo, he would have walked away. Called the governor and told him he had the wrong address. He couldn't even blame her for using a fake name. If the paparazzi had chased him around, he would have changed his name, too. A grin spread across his face at the memory of her feisty response to his insistence. Now *that* would be a story for the grandkids.

Fuck. Grandkids? That meant children. Roger should be heading for the door. Instead, he chuckled to himself, trying desperately not to wake the sleeping spitfire on his chest. He could see a pair of rocking chairs on that big wraparound porch of his, and a swing set in the backyard where he'd taught Caleb how the LARP rules worked. Little kids with tiny foam swords mimicking him and his brothers in garb, while Jenna rolled her eyes and called them in for dinner.

He yawned just thinking about chasing after kids at his age. Maybe Jenna didn't even want kids. He certainly hadn't thought about it in a long time.

Another glance at his phone told him Caleb had sent a text hours ago. He wasn't sure if he'd still be awake, but he didn't want to ignore his sister's boyfriend.

Caleb: It didn't work. The squad totally took over the session and I couldn't work it in.

Roger: Maybe you should have clued them in.

Surprisingly, three dots appeared as Caleb typed a reply.

Caleb: Listen, those girls mean well, and they love Nad dearly, but one of them would have slipped up and said something. They wouldn't mean to, but they would have.

Roger: Okay. Maybe we need a Plan B.

> Caleb: Yeah, I think we do.

> Roger: I'll call you when I'm back in town and we'll come up with something.

> Caleb: Where are you? What about Amber?

> Roger: She's with me. Something happened, and we needed to leave.

> Caleb: Okay. Talk later!

Roger scrubbed a hand over his face and set his phone to Do Not Disturb. Who would have thought, after the way he and his brothers had treated Caleb, that he'd be helping the man plan his proposal? No one. Least of all, Nadia.

He grinned as he remembered her explaining that Caleb was sharing her tent at Armageddon and telling them to put their tents on the other side of Melberth's camp. *"Your sister isn't quiet,"* she'd said. They'd just about thrown Caleb in the trebuchet. No one would ever accuse his sister of being a lady, that was for sure.

Even when Caleb abandoned her, which Roger still didn't fully understand, she'd spit tacks when he, Jon, and Finn got pissed. She blamed herself for the miscommunication and, after time and distance from the incident, he had to agree with her. He almost hung up on Caleb the next time they spoke, when he called to say someone had taken Nadia.

Roger would absolutely keep Caleb's secret, because he hoped someone would do the same for him someday. And by assisting with the proposal, he'd prove to his sister that her brothers had accepted her partner.

Could they accept Jenna as well after his stint as her bodyguard? He smiled, thinking of more Sunday dinners at his parents' house with her at his side. She'd loved his family, and they had welcomed her with open arms as his client.

As sleep overtook him again, he pressed a kiss to the top of her head and closed his eyes.

For the first time in forever, he could see a future with someone.

Chapter 18

Jenna woke to a hard body under her cheek and some-one calling her name.

"Wake up, baby."

She groaned and rolled onto her back, blinking her eyes open. "Coffee?"

"I'll get it started."

Sitting up in the bed, she rubbed the sleep from her eyes and yawned. "Why do we need to get up?"

Roger hauled himself out of bed, and she watched his naked ass walk to the coffeepot. Damn, she wanted to bite it. His butt, not the coffeepot.

"I have a friend who helps me out once in a while. He investigates cybercrimes for the FBI."

The hairs on the back of her neck stood on end. She gulped. "Sounds serious."

"It is. He ran through the code for the security cameras I had hooked up to your apartment the day it was broken into. I got a message that he found something."

"Does he know who did it?"

"I don't know. He wants to do this over video call. He has a way of encrypting it."

Damn. Eraser X would love to meet this guy. Jenna whistled as Roger turned around and she got the full-frontal view.

"Later." He winked. She found herself smiling back at him and understanding what the phrase "give me butterflies" meant. Jenna would definitely miss that sexy smirk.

After they'd both taken turns in the bathroom and dressed for the day, Roger called down to room service to order breakfast and opened his laptop. He pulled Jenna down onto his lap as the video connected.

"Roger!"

"What?" He grinned at her innocently. "There's only one desk chair."

She sighed and rolled her eyes as a man with wire-framed glasses and curly blond hair appeared on the screen.

"Roger?"

"Sam, this is Jenna. She also goes by Amber. Jenna, this is Sam Ivers. We served in the Army together."

She glared at him out of the corner of her eye for outing her, but after last night, she was inclined to let it go. At some point, they were going to have to come clean to his family. And probably her coworkers.

She'd just blame it on the media storm that ended her college career, instead of telling them about the syndicate. And then she'd disappear.

She tried to ignore the way her stomach churned at the thought of leaving him.

"Nice to meet you, Jenna."

"Likewise." She had to give the man credit. He didn't flinch at being introduced to Roger's charge while she was seated on his lap.

"What did you find, Sam?" Leave it to Roger to get right down to business.

Sam adjusted his glasses and focused on Roger. "I'm going to be honest. You did me a huge favor, Hunt. That hacker I've been trying to find? Your code had their signature all over it. The FBI is overjoyed that I can get on with my work now."

Jenna furrowed her brows. He'd been looking for this person who hacked Roger's cameras?

Roger scratched his head. "That strikes me as odd. Why would this guy who hacks museums and shit hack my security cameras? Nothing was even taken from the apartment."

"Most likely, they're a hacker for hire, a mercenary. Since the Fox hasn't been stealing anything, I suspect they needed the work."

All the blood drained from Jenna's face as her code name passed Sam's lips. The gears of her mind started turning. If Eraser X had left traces when she hacked the cameras to help Jenna with her heists, and the FBI was looking for them... that meant they were really looking for *her*.

Not to mention the scariest part of all. She'd been right about the syndicate being the ones who'd broken into her apartment.

"Seriously, this broke my stalemate, brother. I can't thank you enough."

"Maybe they'll let you take that vacation soon, then."

The men laughed while Jenna acted like she wasn't the one Sam was searching for. "Alright, who broke into my apartment?"

"That's the problem. There's no rhyme or reason to what this hacker does, and we can't figure out who he works for. Every time I find his signature, it's coming from a different IP address, so he's been impossible to find. I'm trying, though." Sam gave her a sympathetic look, and Jenna's stomach churned. Even Roger's friends were upstanding citizens. His entire world, his life, was out of her league. What would he think if he knew his princess was really the thief?

Someone knocked on the door, and Jenna rose to let Roger answer it. He checked the peephole. "Just breakfast," he said, looking over his shoulder and smiling.

She turned back to the screen. "Jenna, I'm sorry I don't have more answers yet. But we'll figure out who did this to you. Chances are they're linked to whoever threatened your father." Sam expressed his apologies with a sad smile.

Jenna just nodded, standing when Roger came back to the desk. "Keep us posted. Hopefully, we can get this sorted out, then get home."

Sam gave him a brief salute. "I'll be in touch. Stay safe." The video winked out.

"Come on, little Amazon. Breakfast time." He gestured to the tray of food on the small round table behind her.

Her eggs tasted like rubber, and the toast was like ash in her mouth. She choked them down anyway, not wanting to worry Roger.

But the damn man was too perceptive.

"You okay?"

She just looked up at him, then went back to picking at her food.

"Hey." His hand landed on hers, and her gaze shot back up. "You're going to be okay."

She nodded, then offered him an olive branch of sorts. "It's just ... a lot."

He nodded as if he knew and left her alone to eat in silence.

She shouldn't feel as though Eraser had betrayed her. Everyone in the syndicate was out for themselves. Hell, she'd left with no word to her supposed friend. Eraser probably thought Jenna had turned state evidence or something. In their world, snitches didn't get stitches, they got dragged out into the desert and left for the vultures.

Of course, they'd hire Eraser to help with the break-in. She was their best hacker, after all. And Jenna had been one of their best thieves. No way in hell they'd let her go without a fight.

Forget coming clean with Roger's family. She'd been a fool to remain in Baltimore as long as she had.

Raising her eyes, Jenna contemplated the handsome man in front of her. He was in a class all his own, but he wanted her anyway. And Jenna was just selfish enough to want to keep him. If she ran again, could she take Roger with her?

No, he was too close to his family. He'd never leave them after spending all that time in the military.

She feared that if Roger ever discovered the full extent of her past, he would recoil in horror, realizing that she was a far cry from the partner he deserved. He was the type who would eventually settle down, and he deserved that stability from someone who wouldn't drag him into the syndicate's chaos. This couldn't happen again.

Her heart broke a little at the thought of losing him, but Jenna was used to being alone. She could go back to that in a heartbeat. But she didn't want him to lose out on his money from dear old dad, which meant she was stuck until after the election.

Meanwhile, she had to stay out of the syndicate's cross hairs. It wasn't a hardship to spend two weeks on vacation with a sexy man. Even if they could never be more.

Jenna's phone rang in the middle of the night, waking her from a restless sleep. She squinted at the screen and swiped her finger across to answer when she recognized Erin's name.

"Hello?" she croaked.

"Oh my God, Jenna, someone blew up my car!"

She jolted upward, wide awake. "Are you okay?"

"Yeah, I was at ... my friend's place. The car was still at the apartment. I just got a call from the police."

Roger rolled over from facing the wall and stared at her. Jenna tried to ignore the way her heart raced when he turned those intense eyes her way. Her roommate needed her.

She scrubbed at her face.

"Sorry I woke you up. Where are you?"

"I can't tell you that, Erin."

"I know, I know. Sorry. I'm just completely off base with this. I can't believe they blew up my car!"

"I'm so sorry, Erin." This was all her fault. She never should have taken a roommate. Now this sweet girl who'd helped her had paid dearly for it.

"There's nothing you could have done. If there's any-thing I've learned in my line of work, it's that people are assholes."

Jenna huffed a laugh, even as Roger sat up in bed and rubbed his eyes. "What happened?" He asked in a rough, sleep-laden voice that made her lady parts tingle. *Down, girl, this isn't the time.*

"It's Erin. Her car blew up."

His eyebrows shot upward, and he held out his hand. "Let me talk to her."

Jenna scowled at the command. Leopards never changed their spots. "Erin, Roger's here. Do you want to talk to him?"

"Sure, put him on. Gene will probably want to talk to him, too."

"Gene?"

"Uh, Detective Wells." Erin's voice took on a nervous quality.

"You guys are on a first name basis?"

She could hear her roommate bristle. "We do work together, you know."

"Right, right. Ignore me, I'm tired. Here's Roger." She handed the phone over to his outstretched hand.

He promptly hit the button to put it on speaker. "Hi, Erin. What happened?"

"Honestly, I'm not sure. I was staying with my friend and got the call from the cops that someone had reported an explosion on my block. When they investigated, they pulled my license plate from the wreckage."

"Let me pull up the cameras and see if they caught anything."

Oh shit. He was going to kill her. "Actually, Erin and I agreed we should take them down."

"You did what?" His low volume belied the rage on his face.

"Sorry, Roger." Erin took one for the team. "The landlord wasn't happy when he found out they were installed without permission and since we weren't going to be here, we didn't think it would hurt anything. I had no idea they'd blow up my *car*."

Roger's gaze didn't leave her while they listened to Detective Wells murmuring at Erin in the background. What was going on there?

Jenna found herself grateful for the distraction from the explosion. "Again, I'm sorry, Erin."

"Gene says this escalation is normal. Not that it makes it any easier to deal with. I have insurance on the car. Guess I'll be shopping once their adjuster finishes his work. I just wanted to let you know that whoever your dad's enemies are, they're escalating."

"Good thing we're not there." Jenna looked away, anywhere but at Roger. She didn't dare say what was on her mind.

After they hung up with Erin, Jenna lay wide awake in bed. Erin thought this was all due to her father's political strife, but she knew better. This was absolutely a syndicate intimidation move. And Erin had been the victim. How could she have willingly put an innocent in danger like this?

The last time Jenna had any friends, they'd only really been good for a fun night out. She hadn't bothered to study for her classes since she hadn't had any say in what she studied. The crowd she fell into had been interested in drinking and dancing their cares away. Even though Jenna had tried to keep Erin at arm's length, she'd turned into a real ride-or-die friend. How the hell had *that* happened?

On the plus side, all evidence pointed to the syndicate not knowing she'd left the city. That bought them time. Jenna mentally counted the cash in her bag left over from her last job for the syndicate. Once she got back to Baltimore, she'd dip into it to help Erin replace her car. That old thing couldn't have been worth much, and the insurance payment wasn't likely to help with the down payment on a new one. At least then she could assuage some of her guilt before she disappeared again.

Baltimore wasn't safe, but to keep up appearances, she had to go back with Roger. Then she could tell him who she was, watch the disgust come over his face as he told her he never wanted to see her again, pack up her life and disappear again.

Despite how still he was, Roger wasn't sleeping, either. "When were you going to tell me you took the cameras down?"

At his question, Jenna jolted with surprise, then groaned, and rolled to her side to face him. "I don't know. When we got back?" She shrugged. "I didn't think it mattered."

His fist clenched in the space between them. "Damn it, Jenna! Of *course* it matters. Now we won't know who set the car bomb. None of your neighbors have come forward, and frankly, in that part of town, I'm not surprised."

She couldn't help the caustic tone that came out with her next words. "I'm sorry that I didn't want us to get evicted because my dad's a freaking politician." She really wasn't sorry. Erin had done nothing wrong, and she shouldn't lose her security deposit because Jenna's father liked to stick his nose where it wasn't welcome.

He lifted himself up on one arm, just to glare down at her. "For the love of God and all that is holy, Princess, I hope you take your safety more seriously in the future. Honestly, I'm shocked Erin didn't have better sense than to rent there, working as a dispatcher. You'd think someone in law enforcement would value their security more."

Jenna rolled again to lie on her back. "Do we have to do this at the ass crack of dawn?"

"Well, I'm definitely not sleeping after that phone call."

Neither was she. "It's too early to work out, G.I. Joe."

"Princess, I was Special Forces. We smoke the regular G.I. Joes."

Jenna rolled her eyes. "Well, I'm going to get some more sleep." Or at least pretend she was sleeping. She shivered as she pulled the covers up over her shoulders, wishing they weren't arguing right now. It'd be nice to share in his body heat.

"Just let me do my job, Jenna." Roger must be more tired than she realized because he also laid back down and tugged the covers up. When she shivered again, he turned on his side toward her. "Come here."

"What? No."

The covers undulated as he motioned her over. "You're freezing."

"What's your point?"

"Okay, fine." The next thing she knew, Roger was on her side of the bed and scooping her into the little spoon position. Immediately, she soaked his heat into her skin, even though she didn't deserve his concern. Damn, she would miss this when it was all over.

"I'm just worried about protecting you." His gruff voice ran another shiver down her spine, but thankfully he would think it was from the chill.

"I know," she said, settling into his comforting embrace. Jenna closed her eyes, memorizing how it felt to be in his arms, so she could pull it out on those lonely nights in the future. How she wished her life could be different. "Good night, Roger."

"Good night, Princess."

Chapter 19

SOMETHING WAS WRONG WITH his little Amazon.

It hadn't even been twenty-four hours, and she was restless, picking fights with him over everything from what they ordered for dinner to what they watched on the rather limited television offerings. Damn, he missed his streaming services.

The feisty governor's daughter was back, and Roger didn't understand why. He thought they'd connected on a soul level the night they arrived. He'd laid his heart bare, doing everything short of using the L word. But Jenna was acting as though it never happened.

Had that all been one-sided? Well, that figured. Leave it to him to open his heart for the first time in decades to a woman who didn't appreciate it.

He'd give her until election night was over. If this attitude was the real Jenna, he would walk away instead of asking to keep seeing her.

Pinching the bridge of his nose, he gave up on doing any administrative work in their downtime. "What do you *want*, Princess?"

"I'm going nuts in here. I didn't even bring a swimsuit, so I can't go to the pool. Let's go out somewhere, Roger. Before the walls close in on me."

He sighed. "It's not a good idea." But neither was keeping a tiger caged.

"Just a couple of beers and a round of pool. That's all I want." If that would get her to stop whining, he'd do it.

"I have conditions."

She sat up straighter. "Name them."

"One drink. No more. Don't talk to anyone. And we only go to one bar."

"Done." She rolled her eyes as she got up off the bed and dug around in her bag. "And why would I talk to anyone else when I have you, big boy?" She winked at him and carried her clothes into the bathroom to finally change out of her pajamas.

Roger shook his head at the emotional whiplash. Maybe this was just how Jenna dealt with stress? He could work with that.

The question then became, how much stress would his job put her under?

While she showered, he researched the local watering holes, even calling the front desk for a recommendation. The clerk on duty told him about a place not far from the hotel called Clever Shot, where she played pool with her friends in a billiards league. Perfect.

He took his turn in the shower, trying not to think about Jenna naked. She hadn't been receptive to his advances all day. Maybe a night out would be good for her.

The cinder block building his GPS directed him to wasn't much to look at on the outside. It shared a wall with a bowling alley next door, and the parking lot was riddled with weeds. But there were cars and trucks lined up and down the asphalt. Roger pulled the rental into a space and killed the engine.

"How's this look, Princess?"

Jenna grinned from ear to ear, and he found his own smile spreading across his face in response. "Perfect."

He double-checked his weapons and slid out of the driver's seat, only to see Jenna unlock her door. "Hey!"

Her head snapped to look at him. "What?"

"Wait for me."

She crossed her arms, and he took his time strolling around the vehicle. While he did, he noted the exits, the woods along the side of the parking lot, and the places where someone could hide. When he got to her door, she was tapping her fingers along the window ledge.

Opening it, he shielded her body from view. "It's for your safety, Princess."

She rolled her eyes but didn't say anything. "They don't even know I'm here."

"I'd rather be safe than sorry."

He guarded her back while they made their way through the glass doors. The windowless bar was dim but clean, with a row of pool tables in the back. Clusters of people laughed around high-top tables, and some sat at the bar and rooted for whichever sports team was on the screen.

Light fixtures highlighted the blue felted tables. Out of the six of them, only one was occupied. Roger led Jenna to the one in the corner, where he could watch the door easily.

She racked the balls while he took stock of the people in attendance. No one set off his danger senses, but he wouldn't lower his guard. Jenna gestured for him to break, but he shook his head.

"Ladies first."

She smirked. "Been a while since anyone called me a lady."

"Don't get used to it." He grinned as his stomach flipped. It seemed they were getting back to their flirtatious banter. Thank God.

This thing with Jenna might be new, and he might not have done the relationship thing in forever, but he was all in. As he watched her stalk around the table, determining her best shot, he realized he had to tell her. Jenna wasn't the type to read into what he said. She needed upfront, blunt honesty. Especially growing up in a political household like she had.

But given the predicament they'd found themselves in, as bodyguard and principal, he knew it had to wait until the election was over. Then all bets were off, and he'd tell her … somehow. His baby sister and her friends were better with that touchy-feely shit. Maybe they'd help him. After Nadia stopped laughing.

"Stripes," called Jenna as the orange striped ball went into a pocket. "Are we calling pockets?"

"I never play that seriously." He scanned the bar while she took her next shot.

Roger furrowed his brow as Jenna methodically and systematically devastated him at the game. Ball after ball sank into the pockets as he watched with his jaw hanging open. When she lined up her shot to sink the eight ball, he knew he'd been had.

"You're a fucking pool shark!"

She grinned up at him like the cat that got the cream, then made her shot without looking. "There's no money on the table and I didn't fake being bad at it to get you to place a bet. That means I'm not a shark."

"You're something else, that's for sure." He shook his head. "You'd clean up on an Army base."

She shrugged. "Not my scene."

"That's fair." He racked up again. "This time, I'm going to break."

He managed to sink one ball before he scratched, then Jenna took over and cleared the table again. "How 'bout that drink now?"

"Sure thing, Princess." They replaced the equipment and headed over to the bar, his arm around her waist. She seemed back to her usual self now.

When they squeezed into a space at the bar, Roger flagged down one of the bartenders. "What can I get you?"

"I'll have a Coke, and what do you want?" He looked at Jenna.

"I'll take a Corona."

The younger of the bartenders nodded. "You want to start a tab?"

"No, thanks, man." Roger handed over his card for their drinks and signed the receipt when he brought it back. Then he placed Jenna's bottle up on the bar and popped the lid for her. She brought the longneck to her lips and took a long drink.

"Kicking my ass made you thirsty, huh?" He shook his head as the bartender pressed a cold glass of soda into his hand.

She just grinned like the Cheshire cat. "Don't be a sore loser now."

"I'm not a sore loser. I bought your drink, didn't I?"

"You're a gentleman. You would have done it, anyway."

He leaned into her personal space and enjoyed how her pupils dilated. "Baby, I'm clearly not doing something right if you think I'm a *gentle* man."

Her spine stiffened. "Hold my beer, would you? I need to hit the restroom."

He took her drink and followed her with his eyes. Thankfully, he had a clear line of sight to the ladies' room door. As a table emptied, he took it over, sliding onto the bar stool and placing her beer in front of one of the other seats.

What did he say? Things were going well, and then wham! She shuttered, completely closed off from him.

It had to be his reminder that they'd had sex the night before. He thought he was being clever. Apparently not.

Roger drank his soda quickly. His throat was dry as a desert. But then he started to feel ... strange.

Where was Jenna, and why was she taking so long? Who were all these people? Their forms started to morph, their shadows stretching, stretching, sucking out all the light. He locked eyes with the bartender who'd served them. The man was staring, no longer attempting to serve customers or clean glasses or anything. He had one coherent thought. *I think... I think we've been found.* The need to reach Jenna became stronger than anything else.

And then the darkness took him.

Chapter 20

ROGER WAS TOO GOOD for her. Jenna locked herself in a stall and banged her forehead against the door. She'd let him get close again when she meant to pull away. With the syndicate on her tail, it was the safest thing to do.

Sitting down to take care of business, Jenna reminded herself once again why things between them could never be more than sex. She tried to imagine telling him about her past. That the people who broke into her apartment weren't her father's political enemies, but her former associates. Imagining the disgust on his face should be enough to quell the pain from her heart breaking. And if she prepared herself well enough, he'd never know how much it hurt to tell him the truth.

In fact, better to do it now than put it off any longer. Then he would stop flirting and being sweet to her. And once his job for her father was over, she'd be on her way again. It would be easier for both of them.

Jenna washed her hands and faced the mirror over the sink. She could do this. But it had to be in private. Telling him about her former life was far too risky out in the open, like they were here. She'd have to get him to take her back to the hotel. Maybe tell him she didn't feel well?

It wasn't even a lie. She was nauseous just thinking about what she was about to do.

She lingered so long in the ladies' room, putting her metaphorical armor on, that she knew her beer would be warm when she got back to the bar. When she finally emerged, Roger was nowhere to be found.

The bar was fuller now. Perhaps there were just too many people between her and him. But that didn't seem like Roger. He'd be more likely to stand outside the women's room door waiting for her if he thought it was too crowded. She slid around patrons and tables, fighting against the crowd to get back to the bar. But Roger wasn't there.

Spinning around, she looked out over the crowd for him. She should be able to spot a six-foot-tall former soldier. All he had to do was stand up.

Meanwhile, she was only average height. He'd have a harder time finding her.

"Looking for someone?" An older woman asked. She sat on a stool next to Jenna, her voice croaking like she smoked a pack a day.

"My friend was sitting here when I went to go to the bathroom, but I don't see him now."

"Oh, I saw him. Tall guy, brown hair, wearing a camo print shirt?"

Jenna nodded. "That's him."

She leaned over to let Jenna hear her better. "They just took him outside a few minutes ago."

Jenna furrowed her brow. "Outside?"

"Yeah, he was so drunk he couldn't even stand up."

That only confused her for a moment until the wheels in her head started to turn. Roger hadn't been drinking since he started this bodyguard gig. He refused to drink on the job. Which could only mean one thing.

"Thanks. I'll go find his keys."

"Joe will have them. He's down at the end there." She pointed.

Jenna gave her a thumbs up and fought her way through the press of people to the other end of the bar, where the older of the two bartenders was pouring drinks.

"Excuse me," she said. He looked up.

"What can I get you?"

"My friend that they just took outside? He was my ride. I'm sober. I can drive him home."

"I think they already called him a cab. But here are the keys. You can go check."

"Thanks." She caught them in her hand. They were still warm from Roger's pocket. He couldn't be far. "Can't tell you how many times I've had to drive his truck."

Joe nodded as though he understood. "Have a nice night."

"You, too."

She clutched the key to the rental tightly in her fist and waded back through the customers to the door. Breaking into a run, she hurled herself outside into the humid night air.

"Roger?" Looking left, then right, she didn't see anyone. Shit. They had moved him to a secondary location.

If the syndicate had Roger, they were coming for her. She needed to get out of there or she'd never be able to find him.

As she started up the SUV and drove away, she had to wonder, why would the syndicate take him? What could they hope to gain from it?

She didn't delay in getting back to the hotel and locking herself in their room. She even bolted the door and shoved a chair under the handle. Then she started to pace.

Think, Jenna, think. Who could she call to help find him?

Pulling out her phone, she dialed one of her three contacts. Erin picked up right away. "Jenna? What's going on? It's awful late."

"Sorry, were you asleep?"

"No, I'm on my break at work. I'm working a double."

"I need help, Erin. Roger and I were out at a bar just to get a change of scenery. I went to the bathroom, and when I came back out, someone told me he'd been escorted out. That he was so drunk he could barely stand."

"That doesn't sound like Roger."

"Erin, he was only drinking soda!"

"You think he was drugged?"

"I'm sure of it. I got outside, and he wasn't there."

"Shit, Jen—Amber, sorry. Are you safe?"

"Yeah. I talked them into giving me his keys and went back to the hotel. But I don't know how to find him."

"Give me the address of where you were tonight. I can find someone to see if we can look at the traffic cameras."

"You're the best, Erin." Jenna looked up the address to Clever Shot and read it off to Erin. Erin must have returned to her desk early because she heard the telltale clicks of a keyboard.

Her huff of frustration echoed across the line. "I don't have access to anywhere out of *state*, Amber. We would need an agreement with that county, and those things take time."

"We don't *have* time."

"I know. You just should call the local police. They can put out an APB."

"But I already left the bar."

Erin swore under her breath, and Jenna heard her footsteps carrying her back down a hall. She must be going back to the break room. "They might understand your situation if you explain he's your bodyguard and who you are. Hang on a second." Murmuring in the background made Jenna furrow her brow. But Erin didn't take long. "Gene just reminded me there's a mandatory twenty-four-hour waiting period before they'll do anything about a missing person report. I don't know what to tell you."

Damn it all to hell! This was exactly what Jenna had been trying to avoid by distancing herself from him. Obviously, it was too late. Her chest tightened around her racing heart, and she closed her eyes, trying to force herself to think.

"Roomie? Are you okay?"

"Damn it... I'm sorry. I'm so, so sorry."

"Family emergency, boss. I'll take it back to the break room." Erin's footsteps sounded hurried. "You still with me?"

"Yeah, I... I didn't want to tell you this. But this is no missing person case. Roger's in danger. And it's all my fault."

"How is it your fault?" Even Erin's gentle tone couldn't console her. Jenna took a deep breath, then let her confession fly out before she lost her nerve.

"Before I came to Baltimore, I was a member of an organized crime ring."

A sharp inhale was Erin's only response.

"That's why I was using a different name. I dyed my hair, bought a fake identity, left my car, everything. I swear I left no trace. But it seems they found me."

"How do you know?"

"Roger's friend Sam looked at the camera coding from the night of the break-in. He recognized a particular hacker's signature. She used to work with me."

"Oh, my God. And you think that's who—"

"I'm positive, Erin. And he has no idea who he's up against."

"Level with me." Erin's voice dropped to a whisper. "Are we talking about the mob?"

"Not them, but they run their operations similarly. I wanted out, and I thought I could disappear. My father hiring that PI and finding me blew my cover. That's why I was upset when Roger showed up that first day."

Erin was silent for a long time. Jenna was glad she wasn't there to see her face.

"I'll talk to Gene, let him know what's really going on. Keep me posted, okay? I have to clock back in, but I'll keep my phone on my desk. Please text."

"I will. But I think I know what I need to do. I just didn't want it to come to this." She wished her roommate a good rest of her shift, unable to keep the resignation out of her voice.

Jenna stared down at her duffel bag. It sat there on the floor, its secrets taunting her. But the longer she waited, the more time the syndicate had their hands on a good man. She might not be worthy of him, but he sure as hell didn't deserve whatever they were planning.

Dumping her bag out on the bed, she reached inside for the hidden zipper. After the borrowing ex-boyfriend, she'd bought this bag specifically so no one would get their paws on her equipment. It was lined with a fabric that blocked imaging, like an RFID wallet. Completely undetectable. She unzipped it for the first time since her last job. Why she kept the equipment, she didn't know. Maybe part of her knew the Fox would be required once again. Maybe she would always be a villain.

Out came the anti-thermal imaging bodysuit, gloves, and beanie. Her tiny head lamp, her grappling equipment, and her winch. The night vision goggles came next, then her earpiece. She laid everything out on the bed, then sat back in the desk chair and rubbed her hands over her face. Could she do it? Could she reach out to Eraser, who had turned on her? The ear bud that was a direct line to her old hacker accomplice sat in its case. Turning it on would give Eraser her exact location. What if she alerted the syndicate?

But Jenna didn't have access to anyone else who would know where Roger had been taken. Briefly, she remembered him telling her about Sam helping to track Nadia with her phone. Could that be an option? But when she booted up his laptop, it was password protected. Of course. Besides, the syndicate didn't hire amateurs. They would have turned his phone off before leaving the bar.

She didn't have any other options, and she was running out of time. The syndicate would hack him to pieces before the cops could do a damn thing. This had to be a ploy to lure her out. Well, she wasn't going in unprepared.

The Fox was coming out of retirement.

Chapter 21

ROGER'S HEAD THROBBED MERCILESSLY, as if a thousand tiny drums were beating inside his skull. His arms, heavy and unyielding, resisted his attempts to move them. He cautiously attempted to pry open his eyes, only to be met with a blinding, searing brightness that forced him to squeeze them shut once again. What the hell happened?

He walked himself through the last thing he remembered. Jenna had wanted to go out for a drink. She kicked his ass at pool. Then she got a beer, and he got a Coke. Where did they go again? Oh right. Clever Shot. Then she left to go to the bathroom and ... nothing. Why couldn't he remember?

Voices echoed from the next room, and he strained to make out the words.

"Brett, you idiot! That's not the Fox!"

"What do you mean? It's him in the picture!"

"That's her bodyguard! *That's* the Fox!" A slap reverberated, and Roger inwardly winced for whoever was on the receiving end.

His brain quickly put the pieces together. Someone, most likely this Brett fellow, had drugged him and kidnapped him because he'd mistaken him for someone else. That would explain the hangover from hell.

Roger kept pretending he was still unconscious while cataloging his physical predicament. They'd sat him on a chair of some hard material. He couldn't determine what it was made of until he could either open his eyes without pain or move without letting them know he was awake. His biceps were bound to the damn thing, along with his wrists. And if he tensed his ankles, he could feel bindings there.

"What the hell did you do, Brett? Rob a sex store?"

"He's a big guy, Uncle Larry. I didn't want him breaking out if he got awake."

"I'm not even going to ask."

That might explain the fur he felt along his wrist. Taking a chance, Roger opened one eye just a crack, enough to see hot pink fuzzy cuffs holding his wrists down.

His brothers and sister were going to laugh their asses off.

The most unfortunate thing was, Roger knew dozens of ways to kill a man. But every last one required the *use of his hands*.

He had to get back to Jenna. How the fuck was he going to get out of this? And was she safe?

"It's about time, bitch."

Jenna closed her eyes. "Is this line private, Eraser?"

"Come on, you know me. It's encrypted to hell and back. I protect my information better than Fort Knox."

She let out a breath, knowing the syndicate couldn't listen in.

"What did they offer you to come back?"

Jenna shook her head. "Come back? What are you talking about?"

"Well, I assumed that's why you called me."

"I don't understand. The syndicate ransacked my apartment and blew up my roommate's car, and you think they want me *back*?"

Her former heist helper hummed. "Let's put it this way, you're not dead. Clearly, you accepted their offer."

She growled low in her throat. "There's been no offer, Eraser. I was traveling with someone, and they kidnapped him. No one's contacted me unless you count using my roommate's favorite lipstick to write creepy notes on the bathroom mirror."

"What the fuck?"

"Yeah, exactly. Where did they take him?"

Eraser was quiet on the other end of the line, but Jenna could hear her breathing. "Why should I help you, Foxy? You turned against us."

"I didn't turn against anyone, Eraser! I just wanted out."

"They said you went to the Feds."

"I didn't go to the Feds."

She knew Eraser had found the place when she whistled. "Where did you pick up this hunk of man meat?"

Jenna rolled her eyes. "You wouldn't believe me if I told you."

"Come on. Help a sister out."

"You'll have to help me find him first." She paused, try-ing to decide how to entice her former accomplice. "He's got two brothers."

"Mm, no dice, Foxy. If you're not back with us, I can't assist."

"Then at least tell me why, Eraser. Why would they kidnap my friend?"

Eraser clucked her tongue. "Looks like boss-man Lar-ry figured out who you were with. We were tracking his credit card and the hotel charge pinpointed your location. Apparently, his nephew lives in the area and was tapped to pick you up after his bar shift." Her laughter grated on Jenna's nerves. "Did you really think we wouldn't find you?"

She rubbed at the headache trying to form. "That doesn't explain why Roger was the one taken."

A few more clicks of the mouse was the only sign Eraser was still there. "Apparently that idiot just sent a photo without indicating who he wanted in it. It's you and Hot-tie McHotterson."

Jenna groaned. "Please, Eraser, I need to get him out. He's not involved with this."

"He might be persuaded."

She scoffed. "He's a good man. Much better than any of us. He'll never join."

Eraser's tone became somber, all the teasing dropped. "Then he's not going to survive, and you know it."

Over her dead body, damn it! Jenna's temper flared; beneath that black dye was a natural redhead. Her dad used to say she came with a warning label.

Then she got an idea. Even if Eraser called her bluff, she could take Roger's laptop back to Baltimore and find someone to get into it. Then she could contact Sam, who was sure to help.

It was worth a shot.

"Look, Eraser, I didn't want to do this. But I will turn state's evidence if they harm a single hair on that man."

"You'd never get immunity after what you've done. And you'd be signing your death certificate."

Jenna didn't let Eraser deter her. "In fact, he has a good friend who works at the FBI that is looking for you specifically. They could tell it was *you* who hacked the security cameras he put up around my apartment. And if you don't help me get him out of there, all I have to do is get this earpiece to that buddy and you're *all* going down."

Eraser inhaled a sharp breath. "You wouldn't dare."

She certainly would. "I'm done with this organization, and I won't go back. But I won't turn it in if they let me and Roger go."

She didn't know how much time she had for her old colleague to decide.

"Tick-tock, Eraser."

"Fine! I'll do it. But you need to tell me why you wanted out. The money's good, ain't it?"

Jenna kept her talking while she dressed for her mission. For once, she was donning these clothes to do good, instead of steal gems. And she worried if she let Eraser off the line, that she'd change her mind.

"I'm thirty-five, you know. I'm not built to do all this crawling around and stuff anymore. That bullet last year was a wake-up call. I wasn't ready to meet my end on the wrong side of the law." She zipped up the bodysuit, remembering the delicate repair job she'd done to it when a guard from her last target had nearly caught her. Then she tucked her hair up inside the beanie. "Plus, something wasn't right. Where did they get that money? What were they doing with those gems? My gut told me to get the fuck out, so I did."

Eraser was silent.

"You still there?" Jenna checked.

"Yeah, I... I know what you mean. I've come across some... weird files. Coded messages. I haven't been able to crack them yet. But yeah, my gut's been screaming 'Something's wrong' at me, too."

Interesting. Jenna laced her boots and tucked the gloves into her pocket. On instinct, she packed up all their things. If she and Roger had to make a run for it, he wouldn't want to leave his laptop behind. Better safe than sorry. Her night vision goggles and her other equipment stayed in the top section of the bag this time.

She carried everything out to the SUV, Eraser still in her ear. Although she only knew that because she could hear the fans that kept her overpowered computer cool. Once she got into the vehicle and started it up, she spoke again.

"I'm ready. Are we doing this?"

"Yeah. Yeah, I'll help you get your man out." She tsked. "This must be some grade-A dick for you to risk your life like this."

Jenna didn't bother to correct her on Roger being her man. "Alright. Which direction am I going?"

Eraser led her through a series of twists and turns into an industrial district for the small town they'd ended up in.

"There's no camera on this side of the building. It's an access road that isn't in use anymore."

"Thank you for that assurance," she bit out, her teeth grinding as the SUV bumped over the road. With no head-lights. Because stealth.

She didn't miss this part a bit.

"I just wanted to explain why I took you this way. That's all, Foxy." Eraser sounded contrite.

"Just be glad you're not riding along in person," Jenna grunted.

"Alright, that brick warehouse coming up at twelve o'clock is the one you want. Don't park too close."

"Got it." She edged the vehicle off the side of the glorified trail and parked it behind a copse of trees. Before she got out, she strapped the rest of her gear on, then grabbed some big branches from the woods and leaned them up against the SUV. The last thing she needed was the glint from someone else's headlights giving away her position.

While she hefted her camouflage into place, Eraser surprised her. "You know, if you'd come to me, I could have helped you get out."

She faltered, almost dropping the branch she held. "What?"

Eraser made a humming noise that might have accompanied a shrug. "I got skills, you know."

"The point was no one was supposed to know."

"I just mean, we've worked together for years. I thought we were friends, so when Larry said you turned on us, it... it hurt, you know? I might not have understood at the time, but I could have helped you disappear. Wipe your information from the records so it was like the Fox never existed."

Jenna swallowed against the lump in her throat. "I'm sorry. I didn't realize I could..."

"You didn't think you could trust me?"

She snorted. "I saw too many people stabbed in the back." After a beat of silence, she shook her head and turned toward the building. "I'm really sorry, Racer."

"Naw, it's okay. I get it. They don't even let us exchange names. They don't want us to trust each other."

Jenna nodded, even though Eraser couldn't see her. Sliding her night vision goggles in place, Jenna creeped towards the building. "Let's save the sappy stuff for later. What's my entry point?"

"See that door with the keypad?"

"Yeah."

"When the light turns green, that means I've disabled the security system."

"Alright."

"Just answer me one more thing first, Foxy." Eraser's exasperation was evident. "What's so special about this guy, huh? Why is he worth leaving the syndicate and risking your neck?"

Jenna took a precious second to consider her answer. How could she explain to Eraser that Roger had too much integrity to join the syndicate? That she'd never want him to taint himself the way she'd been tainted?

In the end, and in the interest of time, she went with the simplest answer she could. "He's a good guy, Eraser. Better than I deserve."

Eraser chuckled, and Jenna could hear her grin come through the phone. "But you're a bad enough bitch to take him, anyway." A clap sounded on Eraser's end. "Alright, Foxy, let's do this. One last run, for old time's sake."

"Eraser? Call me Jenna."

Another giggle. "And you can call me Frankie."

Chapter 22

"How do you know the Fox?"

"I have no idea who you're talking about." Roger yawned to show this guy how bored he was. Although he really was getting tired of this line of questioning. Once he'd decided to let his captors know he was awake, he'd had to deal with the not-quite-an-apology from this guy who appeared to be in charge. "Can a guy get a drink around here?"

"And how exactly would you drink it? We're not letting you out of those cuffs."

He cocked an eyebrow at this Larry dude. Larry looked to be about fifty or sixty, with a balding head and a beer belly. He was absolutely the brains of the operation here, knowing better than to release a guy who could kick his ass ten ways to Sunday.

Roger sighed, slipping into his anti-interrogation training from his army days. The funny thing was, he really had no idea who this Fox person was. Except it sounded like whoever Sam was searching for, Roger had been mistaken for them.

Too bad they'd taken his cell. He'd love to let Sam know where these assholes were hiding. Although it sounded like Fox wasn't with them.

"Look, man, I don't know who you're talking about. I was on a date with a girl, we were getting drinks and next thing I know, I'm here."

Larry held his hand out to Brett, who slapped a folder into it. The old guy thumbed through the pages inside. "Roger Hunt, formerly of the US Army Special Forces, served twenty years and retired. I'm sure with a bit more digging, we could get your military records." *He can try,* Roger thought wryly. He thumbed through a bit more. "Owner and operator of Hunt Security. What exactly are you doing here in Florida when your business is in Maryland?"

Roger remained silent.

Larry closed the folder, tucking it under his arm. "Look, we just want the Fox, okay? She needs to come back to work. You can sit there and let us know when you're ready to talk."

Then he stomped away, his frustration on display. Brett, who Roger remembered as the younger bartender at Clever Shot, hurried after him.

They shut the lights in the room out and locked the door.

Submerged in darkness, Roger's headache finally started to ease. He'd been squinting at those idiots. He really needed some water to help with the dehydration their drug had caused.

He knew how these usually went. Hell, at least they hadn't started the torture yet.

Now that he was alone, Roger slipped his fingers around the cuffs. If they were in fact sex store cuffs and not real ones covered in pink feathers, he'd be fine. The only sound in the storage room they were keeping him in was the bang of the heating system coming on.

Until he heard a faint noise coming from the ventilation shaft above his head. Looking up from where he was trying to undo the cuffs, he watched as the metal grate lifted away and into the ceiling. Then, a figure emerged wearing black from head to toe, lowering herself down to the floor on a rope. Her eyes hid behind night vision goggles, but he'd know that set of curves anywhere.

"The fuck are you doing here?" he whispered. She put a finger to her lips and shook her head.

This wasn't safe! But... where did she get that kind of equipment, anyway? She looked like a professional cat burglar.

Wait just a second... They'd asked him about Fox, who he knew from Sam was a jewel thief. Larry slipped and said Fox was female just now. Jenna had been living under a fake name. And from the photos her father had sent him, she'd undergone a drastic makeover.

He blinked, his fight with the cuffs forgotten. Brett had mistaken him for Jenna? Because it *was* Jenna they were after, wasn't it?

His chest puffed out even as his ears started to ring. The sight of her coming to his rescue should emasculate him, but all he felt was pride. And a hefty dose of fear. Which was the only thing keeping his cock at half-mast.

The sexy little catsuit really did it for him.

Roger opened his mouth to ask her if his theory was correct as she padded over to him, and she placed a gloved hand over it, shaking her head firmly. Fine. They could discuss it once they got out of there.

She dropped to her knees and opened the cuffs around his wrists. Silently laying them on the floor, she pulled a pocketknife from somewhere and clipped the zip ties that held his ankles to the chair. She stood then and gestured for him to get up. Roger shook his head, lifting his hands to show her his upper arms were bound as well. She quickly clipped those zip ties as well, her frantic glances at the door setting him on edge.

Her rope was still dangling down from the ventilation shaft. Roger tugged on it, testing the weight. She clipped a belt around both of them that was attached to the rope and held onto him. He shook his head. This was going to be a tight fit.

The whir of a winch made him glance down at Jenna. Slowly, the harness began to rise with them in it. She bit her lip. The sounds the machine made sounded strained. He wondered if it would get them up there or drop them to the floor.

Just as they were about to reach for the hole in the ceiling, the lights came on, blinding them both. Jenna swore as a gun fired, and they plummeted to the floor.

Roger barely had time to make sure he cushioned her fall. Damn, his back was going to feel that for days. Jenna swore a blue streak, her hand over her goggles. Roger lifted them, knowing from experience how wearing those in the daylight could blind you. She only gave him a moment to stare into those baby blues before her mouth set in a firm line and she stood up between him and the guys Larry had brought in this time.

ADRENALINE RACED THROUGH JENNA'S veins, the hairs on the back of her neck standing at attention. Larry stood at the door, a tiny trail of smoke rising from the pistol in his hand. He handed it off to one of the gorillas at his side as he stepped forward.

"Well, well, well. I should have known you'd turn up."

Jenna didn't let her eyes wander, but she felt Roger stand behind her, guarding her back. "It's impolite to kidnap people. If you wanted a date with him, you should have swiped right."

Larry laughed in a loud, honking bray she hadn't missed one bit. "About that. There seems to have been a miscommunication with my nephew. Apparently, he thought Roger was you."

She fought the urge to roll her eyes. It was a common enough misconception that such a high-ranking jewel thief must be a man. Whenever those people learned she was the Fox, there was always shock and awe. It annoyed her to no end.

Larry's gesture at one henchman at his side made her look, but only for a moment. She recognized him as the younger of the bartenders at Clever Shot. So they'd had a plant.

"We haven't been in town that long, Larry. How'd you know where we'd be?"

"Well, for starters, your old pal Eraser hacked the airline manifest."

A whisper came over the earpiece Jenna had hidden in her ear. "Sorry, Foxy."

She gave no outward indication that Eraser was in her ear. "How is Eraser?"

"We're keeping her busy."

Eraser muted herself but not before Jenna heard her snort. It had always been simpler this way; Eraser could hear everything and watch over the security cameras she'd hacked, but she wouldn't distract Jenna from her mission.

"I didn't come here to catch up, Larry."

That made Larry sneer. "It was supposed to be *you* in that chair, Fox."

She smirked. "Funny how things work out sometimes, isn't it?"

Her light tone only pissed him off more. Oh, how that red face used to intimidate her. Now it just amused her because she knew he'd get sloppy.

But that left two unknowns in the room. Jenna didn't like unknowns.

"I have an offer for you from the big bosses."

"I told you, I'm too old to do this shit on a regular basis anymore. That was my last job."

"You don't get to decide that, Jenna O'Malley."

Yeah, she'd given her real name when she joined back when she was young and stupid, not that they wouldn't have figured it out. The fact he was using it meant he was serious. Syndicate members never used real names, even if they knew it. Most members didn't know each other's real names. Larry was likely a fake name he'd taken on when he joined.

But she wouldn't let him see her sweat. "Larry, in all seriousness, my father received death threats. You're not the only one looking for me. Now I'm done here."

"There wouldn't have been any death threats if you hadn't tried to walk away."

Now he had her attention. "What the hell do you mean?"

The satisfied smirk on Larry's face made her gut churn. "We always knew who your father was, Fox. The syndicate made those threats to smoke you out. The big bosses knew even if you didn't come running when Daddy called, he'd move heaven and earth to find his precious little girl."

Those sick fucks. Her father had played right into their hands.

"Was that supposed to scare me? Bringing my parents into it? Come on. You know me better than that."

"It certainly would have been a nice side effect." Larry's grin made her skin crawl. "Now, back to business. They ordered me to bring you back. Your resignation is not accepted." He adopted a sickeningly sweet tone. "I'll even let you keep your little pet if you come back quietly."

Roger tensed behind her, the only sign he was affected. "What if he can't make the move to Vegas?"

"Then he dies." Larry's familiar snarl returned, and her heart dropped. There was no choice. They *had* to get out. "Whether *you* live depends on your work ethic." He turned to stalk away. "Tie them both up."

No way in hell was she letting Tweedledum and Tweedledee follow through on that. Jenna dropped into a defensive stance even as she continued acting. "Sounds kinky." The two musclemen started heading their way, the bartender plant pulling a hank of rope out of his back pocket. Once Larry left the room, she scowled at them. "But I'm not interested."

When the guy she'd never seen before lunged for her, she slapped the gun from his hand and nailed him in his flabby gut. He let out a groan and swiped at her, but she dodged it easily, slamming an elbow into his kidney.

While that was happening, Roger had engaged the bartender in a wrestling match, trying to get the rope away from him. He grappled with him, their bodies twisting and contorting in a fierce struggle for control.

Jenna spied the gun on the floor and reached for it, only for a booted foot to connect with her hand. Tweedledum, she had decided on a name, had recovered, and was coming for her. Before she could retaliate, he'd shoved her toward Roger and his opponent.

Everyone went down in a tangle of chaos and grunts. Then she and Roger found themselves straining against the bartender's strength.

Their fingers desperately clawed at the rope that the other man had tightly wrapped around their arms. Sweat poured down her face, blurring her vision, but she refused to give up. No way would she be a prisoner of the syndicate again, and she'd never let them have Roger.

With a burst of strength, Roger managed to overpower their opponent, ripping the rope free from the bartender's grasp. Triumph surged through her veins as he held the rope triumphantly aloft, a victorious smile spreading across his face as the rope fell from her arms.

Before they could revel in their victory, the click of a gun safety made them both freeze. "Nobody. Move." They turned their heads to see the other henchman panting and sweating like a horse with the gun trained on her. He looked at Roger. "You're going to let Brett tie you up like a good boy, or she pays the price."

Chapter 23

Roger swallowed hard, an icy chill sending shivers down his spine. It had been a long time since he'd had a gun trained on him, and never on someone he cared about this much.

But he didn't miss a beat. He slipped a hand behind his back to where he kept his secondary pistol and whipped out his NAA Mini-Short. "You'll be dead before you pull the trigger."

"Where the fuck were you keeping that?"

"You were supposed to search him, asshole!" The nameless henchman roared.

Brett glared at him. "I've never done this before!"

Jenna snorted at him. "Virgins."

Just then, the door crashed inward on its hinges as a dozen men with shields and Kevlar vests burst through the opening. "Police!"

Roger and Jenna held their hands up, Roger stooping to place his tiny pistol on the ground. Someone must have tipped them off because they only tackled Brett and his accomplice. Then he saw Larry being led away in cuffs, his face red as he spat and sputtered.

"Sir? Ma'am? Do we need to call an ambulance?"

"I'm fine, Officer. Although I could use the bathroom," Roger replied, then looked at Jenna. "Are you okay after that fall?"

"I'm fine." Her expression guarded. Roger realized she might not be comfortable around the authorities.

"Great. Come with me and we'll get your official statements." He didn't take them far, only over to the side of the room, out of the way while the boys in blue took care of the men who'd help hold him hostage.

Roger explained exactly what had happened at the bar, from when he'd realized Brett had drugged him. Jenna filled in the blank spots, explaining how she'd gotten his keys from the other bartender and gone back to the hotel when she realized she'd lost him.

"I needed to get back to my tech to contact someone and find out where he'd been taken."

As she told her side of the story, Roger wondered who she'd called.

"Your tech?" The officer looked perplexed.

Roger produced his card. "She's been working with me at Hunt Security."

The cops had slipped that the video didn't have any sound, and they hadn't been sure what they were walking into. Brett had squealed like a pig. Roger had heard him blame everything on his uncle Larry, even mentioning the death threats to get sympathy. Or a plea deal. Somehow he hadn't mentioned that Jenna was the Fox. Probably because he didn't actually know who that was, or why it might be important. Roger was just grateful he was a moron.

Once the officer had everything he needed, he explained they were free to go. If they were needed to testify in court, the department would be in contact. "But honestly, it's pretty cut and dried. The DA won't have any problems getting a conviction with the camera footage your friend sent to us, even without sound." He paused. "I'll also send a report over to the Santa Fe police department. I'm sure they'll be interested in who was making those threats to the governor."

Roger shook his hand gratefully. "I think our little vacation is over, then. Thank you very much." Thank God they'd bought his story about why she had the equipment. He wouldn't release his breath until they were out of there, though. The cops couldn't know about Jenna's history.

As they made their way outside into the night lit up with red and blue flashing lights, Jenna led him around the side of the building to where she'd hidden the rental. She unlocked it and handed him the keys, then slid into the passenger seat when he opened her door. Only then did he see the tension start to leak out of her shoulders.

"You." He stared at her, her sweaty hat hair, her black catsuit that was more practical than sexy, and knew he'd never seen anyone more beautiful. Here was a woman who could not only handle danger but laughed in its face. She was perfect. She was everything. She was... his. And it was time to let her know it. "You were incredible."

She grinned. "So were you. Where the hell were you hiding that little thing? Your ass crack?"

Roger snorted. "No. A special holster under my shirt." He leaned in and cupped her face, then pulled back when her eyes shuttered and she turned away. "Jenna?"

She shook her head, dislodging his hand. "You don't want me."

"The hell I don't!" He nearly roared. But this was no place to have this discussion. He shut her door, then stormed around to the driver's side. Hopping in, he fired up the engine. They'd go back to the hotel to discuss it in private.

Luckily, she didn't make him wait that long. "I'm not a good person, Roger. I'm a fucking criminal."

"You're a fucking badass. My dick's hard enough to hammer nails right now."

"Roger…" Her voice trailed off as they drove slowly past the police vehicles in the front of the building. She pulled something out of her ear, and hit a button, then zipped it into a pocket of her catsuit.

"Was that an earpiece?"

"Yeah. I wanted privacy for this."

"Who was listening?"

She stayed silent long enough that he wondered if she was going to answer him. "A friend." Her lip curled up at one side. "Apparently, she sent the live video feed to the local cops. She said if I didn't want you, she'd come ride you like a roller coaster."

He chuckled as he drove along the dark highway, a million questions crowding his mind. But only one snuck out of his mouth. "Why do you think I don't want you?" Fuck. Hadn't it just been last night he'd made love to her?

One hand rose to press into her sternum, and her breath hitched. "You — you shouldn't. This whole kidnapping thing just proves it. You deserve better than me."

"Baby, we went over this just last night. I wasn't a good guy. I was just following orders." He let that sink in for a moment. "You've been very loud about protesting my following you around since I showed up at your apartment. Yet when you had the chance to cut and run, you came for me. I might be good, but there was no way I was going to walk out of there in one piece by myself."

She winced. "They're why I was against you following me around. I knew anyone who got too close to me could be a target. I didn't expect them to mistake you for me, but that Brett guy was a total noob and just didn't know any better."

"Honestly, it's good that he did. Because I never could have gotten you out if that had been you in that chair. How did you find me, anyway?"

"My friend... she told me where they took you. And she helped me by disarming the security alarm."

"Your hacker friend? The one Sam's been hunting? The one that hacked my cameras so these people could break into your apartment?"

She grimaced. "That's the one."

"I'm really glad it all worked out, but *what in the actual fuck, Jenna*?" He roared. "She could have turned on you!"

"I didn't have a choice. I didn't have your password to get a message to Sam."

Well, damn. "It was still risky."

"Would you have rather I let them kill you?"

What could he say to that?

"All's well that ends well," he huffed.

Jenna grabbed onto his arm as he came up to their hotel. "We can't stay here."

"Why?"

She grimaced. "They tracked your card. And there's more where those assholes came from."

Roger mulled this over. "Alright. Looks like I better find an ATM." He kept on driving, resolving to call the hotel and check out over the phone.

At a truck stop along the highway, Roger withdrew a couple hundred in cash. Then he drove back toward the airport.

"Will we be safe to fly?"

"Eraser's the only one I know of who can hack the airline computers. And she's on our side now. She's going to make sure all my information disappears from the syndicate's files. They won't know I exist."

"Alright." Despite the huge lie of omission, Roger knew in his gut he could trust his little Amazon. Thinking back to the first time they saw each other outside of the LARP, all her actions made sense. In her own way, she was trying to protect him just as he wanted to protect her.

Silence reigned as he pulled into the parking lot of the first hotel he could find, off the beaten path, and unlikely to ask questions. He put the SUV in park and turned to face her. "You saved me when you didn't have to. I don't know who you used to be, but the person you are now is pretty fucking incredible. And a good one, too."

Yellow lights from the hotel illuminated her face in the darkness as she turned to him. Her lips mashed together for a moment as her wide, open gaze met his. "Before I went in there, my friend asked why it was so important to get you out. And I told her, 'He's a good guy, Eraser. Better than I deserve.' And she said, 'But you're a bad enough bitch to take him, anyway.'"

Roger grinned as he stared down into her sapphire eyes.

"I guess if you're not running, I won't either." Jenna smirked back at him.

"If you tried, I'd throw you over my shoulder, tie you to my bed and convince you to stay."

She shivered. "Can we revisit the bondage idea in a while? It's too close to home right now."

"Whatever you want." He reached across the console and cupped the back of her head, hovering his face an inch from hers. "I can't wait to get you out of that sexy little catsuit."

She nipped his bottom lip and slipped from his hold. "Last one to the shower blows the other."

"I'm about to be the happiest loser you've ever seen, Princess."

Her eyes widened, but she bolted out of the rental just the same. Whistling, Roger reached for their bags in the back and locked the car with a beep. Then he sauntered into the lobby to book a room.

Jenna grabbed the key as soon as they had the room number and he followed at a leisurely pace. When he got into the room, the bathroom door was open just a crack; the air growing hot and humid as the sound of the water running filled the room. He slipped the "Do Not Disturb" sign on the front knob, then locked the door and slid the deadbolt home. Tossing their bags toward the bed, Roger opened the bathroom door and heard movement behind the curtain. He stripped at a leisurely pace, imagining all the ways he wanted Jenna tonight and every night.

They had all the time in the world.

"You coming?"

"Not for a little bit," he teased as he stepped into the tub. Jenna leaned her head backward into the water and rinsed out her shampoo. "You're definitely coming first."

He lowered himself to his knees and encouraged her to lean against the wall and hold on to the handle in the shower. Lifting one of her legs, he slid it over his shoulder and trailed open-mouth kisses up her inner thigh. When he stopped short of where he knew she wanted his mouth, he chuckled at her whine. Then he gripped her thighs and gave them what they both wanted.

Burying his face in her red curls, Roger feasted on her pussy. He thrust his tongue into her hole and then pulled back to flick her clit with his tongue. Over and over and over. Soon she was moaning and riding his face. He could feel her walls quiver around his tongue, and he slipped two fingers inside and curled them up just right. Then she exploded, crying out and spasming around his digits.

He slowly brought her down with gentle caresses and soft licks. He'd have taken her up for another orgasm, but the water turned ice cold. Then she was shrieking for a different reason. Steadying her when she tried to hop off his face, Roger reached out and flipped the faucet off.

"Best earmuffs ever, Princess. Can I wear you all winter?" He smirked, looking up at her flushed face and heaving chest.

"Might get a bit awkward in public."

He shrugged. "Too bad." Standing up, he lifted her into his arms and carried her out of the shower and set her down on the counter. Then he wrapped one of the hotel towels around her and gently dried her off before drying himself off with a different towel.

She tried to jump off the counter, but Roger was too quick. Hoisting her up over his shoulder, he smacked that curvy ass and watched it jiggle in the mirror. "Hey!"

"Nope. You're mine, little Amazon." Her protests subsided as he carried her out to the bed. Before he could flip her onto it, her teeth dug into his ass cheek.

"Ooh! You naughty little thing." He tossed his tiny, curvy prisoner onto the bed and followed her down, caging in a laughing Jenna.

"And you're a Neanderthal."

"I'm *your* Neanderthal, and don't you forget it." He nipped at her breast and licked the sting away.

"Really?"

Roger looked up from her chest, and seeing the vulnerability in her gaze, he sobered up.

"Really, Jenna." He lifted himself up to plant a kiss on her lips. "I don't care who you used to be. You made a choice to leave it behind and I respect that. It couldn't have been an easy thing to do. All I care about is who you are now."

"I don't want to be that person anymore."

"Who do you want to be, then?"

She looked away, then back at him. "Worthy."

Roger furrowed his brows in confusion. "Of what?"

Jenna squirmed under him and dropped her gaze. "Of you. Your... l-love."

Cupping her face, Roger turned it up to face him again. "You have it." He grinned at the shock on her face. "I wasn't going to say anything. I thought it was too soon."

Tears welled up in her eyes, and her lips tripped over her next words. "Say it for me?"

He pressed his forehead against hers. "I love you, Jenna O'Malley."

"I — I love you too, Roger Hunt."

Unable to hold himself back any longer, Roger claimed her mouth and showed her just how much.

Chapter 24

AFTER HOURS OF LOVEMAKING and hot, sweaty sex, Roger had convinced Jenna of his feelings. Was she worthy? Fuck, no. But like Eraser had said, she was bad enough to take him, anyway.

Sated but still wired after their ordeal, Roger and Jenna lay awake in bed, talking.

"What's your next move?"

"What do you mean?"

"Do you want to go back to the Urban Roadhouse?"

She shook her head. "I don't think they want me back after all the issues. And besides, waiting tables does *not* pay that much. I need a better job."

Roger ran his fingers through her hair. "You should come work with me."

"What?" She sat up to get a better look at him, snatching the sheet back up over her breasts when his gaze dropped. "Are you serious?"

Scowling for a moment at where the sheet covered her chest, he nodded. "Yeah. I can help get you a concealed carry permit. I need the help anyway." He sat up and leaned against the headboard.

"You're serious." She tried to think of herself as a security woman. To be honest, Jenna hadn't made plans that far ahead in years. She'd been so focused on survival, first in the syndicate, then on the run from them, that her next move hadn't occurred to her. Everything had revolved around escaping her poor decisions.

"Yeah. Unless you're not interested." He shrugged. "If you don't want the responsibility, I could use some help with the administrative stuff. It'd be nice not to do everything."

"You mean even though my dad specifically asked for you to be my bodyguard, you didn't have anyone else to do it, anyway?" Roger nodded. "That's insane."

He shrugged. "That's life as a small business owner."

Jenna shook her head. "I'll think about it."

"Let me know." His hand stroked up and down her back, and Jenna relaxed into him. "As soon as this election's over, I'm taking you on a date."

She smiled and pulled him down to lay on the bed, sleep coming at last. "I'm looking forward to it."

ERIN PICKED UP ON the first ring. "Jenna! Are you okay?"

"Yeah, we're fine. I got him out, and the people who took him are behind bars."

"Are you going to find another place to lie low?"

"No, we're coming home. It turns out those assholes were the ones making the threats in the first place. I have a friend on the inside who's going to make my information disappear. They won't find me again." Eraser had been happy to make Jenna disappear. Maybe she should have reached out for help in the first place. But then, she might not have been stuck with Roger as a bodyguard.

"How's Gene?"

"Um, what?"

Jenna smirked. "Detective Wells?"

"Oh, uh, he's ... he's fine." Erin stammered, tripping over her words.

"Where have you been staying? With your parents?"

"N-no. I did the first night, but after the car exploded, Gene thought it would be best if I stayed at his place."

Jenna let out a wolf whistle, which only flustered her roommate more.

"It wasn't like that! He has a guest room." Jenna waited for Erin to continue. "He's too old for me."

"Hey, I won't judge you."

"There's just one problem with you coming back."

Jenna hummed and let Erin change the subject. "What's that?"

"The police haven't taken the yellow tape down from our door yet. We still can't live there."

"Shit." She thought her response would be lost in the background noise of the airport, but Roger turned toward her, anyway. His ears were attuned to her frequency, as if they were made for each other. Sweet, but a bit creepy at the same time.

"Thanks for the heads up. I'll let Roger know." Where could she go?

"I'm sorry, Jenna."

"Oh, my God. I should be apologizing to *you*! This all happened because of who I used to be."

"It's okay, really."

Jenna scrubbed a hand down her face. "It's not, but I appreciate you saying that."

"Hey." Her friend's voice softened. Jenna plugged her other ear so she could hear. "You got out. You wanted a different life. Their actions are on *them*, not you. They could have just let you go."

She snorted. "They don't typically operate that way." Even now, the only way Jenna knew she'd be safe was thanks to Eraser, who was living up to her hacker name and eliminating all traces of Jenna from the syndicate's history.

After explaining who Eraser was and what her plan was, Roger had kindly extended an invitation to her friend to come to Baltimore when she'd erased herself from their system as well. Eraser, or rather, Frankie, said she'd be there once she finished her own investigation. With Jenna revealing that she was traceable, Frankie had said she wanted to get all the dirt possible on the syndicate to make sure she wouldn't have to go back into their systems.

"I know. But you get my point."

"Yeah." Just then, their boarding announcement came over the airport loudspeaker. "I'll see you when I get back. We can meet for coffee and catch up."

"Sounds great. Text me when you get home."

Home. It had been so long since Jenna had let herself consider some place home. Calling Baltimore home felt right.

"What's up?" Roger asked as she put her phone away.

"Erin says we can't go back to the apartment yet. The cops still have the caution tape up."

Roger rubbed the back of his neck. "Stay with me."

"Pardon?" She crossed her arms and sat back. "I can get a hotel or something."

Jenna held back her laugh as he scowled at her. Man, he was fun to tease. "I'm still your bodyguard until the election. And you'll be safer at my house. I have the best security system on the market and it's free."

"Well, I can't beat the price." She smirked. "But that sounded like an order."

He sighed and closed his eyes, giving his head a shake but smiling. Then he held his hand out and waited for her to put hers in it. "Would you like to stay with me?"

"Hmm. Would I get my own room?"

He shrugged, but he couldn't fully hide his disappointment. "If that's what you want."

She leaned forward. "It's not."

He grinned. "I would have had fun convincing you, but this makes it easier."

They stood when their section was called and headed for the line. Roger didn't let go of her hand, and Jenna found it comforting. She hadn't thought she'd ever have this kind of life.

"Are you going to be okay on the flight?" he murmured.

"Yeah, I'll be fine."

Roger gave her a sheepish look. "I couldn't charter a plane."

"That's not why I was freaking out before." She pulled out her ticket as they moved forward in line. "I realized the syndicate could have planted someone at the airport to follow us. And I spent the entire time being paranoid." He squeezed her hand.

"I'm sorry I wasn't more sympathetic. It didn't even cross my mind."

"Why would it? You had no idea they were after me at the time." She squeezed back to reassure him. She paused the conversation while the gate attendant scanned their boarding passes and wished them a pleasant flight.

Halfway down the walkway, she turned and continued in a hushed voice. "Turns out, Frankie hacked the airline computers, and that's how they knew where to find us."

Roger smacked his forehead with his palm. "And we just happened to be close to Larry's nephew when we found that bar."

"Yeah," she murmured as they made their way down the ramp to the plane. "You know," Jenna said as they found their seats. "I had no idea he had any family."

Roger shrugged and lifted their bags into the overhead compartment. "He probably kept it quiet for the same reason you did."

She nodded. "Most likely. If Larry was even his real name."

They sat down, Roger giving her the window seat again, and buckled in. "When we get back, I want to meet Erin for coffee. We have stuff to catch up on."

"Like what?"

"Well, like us." She waggled her eyebrows. "And apparently she's been staying with Detective Wells throughout this whole thing."

"Really?" His brows shot to the top of his forehead.

"Yup. She slipped and called him Gene. Apparently, they're on a first name basis."

He made a dismissive gesture with his shoulder. "Well, they do work together."

"Yeah, but I think there's something there. Just wait and see."

"Okay, Princess." His lip curled up in a grin. "I'll be interested to see this."

Chapter 25

Roger pulled the bag of microwave popcorn out when it beeped and poured the steaming snack into a bowl. He grabbed two beers from the fridge as well, then he walked over to his living room, where the brand-new couch had been taken over by Jenna, Gene, and Erin. He placed the bowl on the coffee table and handed Jenna her beer, since their guests already had theirs.

Then he kicked back in his old recliner, which up until a week ago had been the only furniture in front of his big screen television. On the screen was a map of New Mexico, broken up by county lines. Different sections of the state were red, others were blue, and some of them were gray, showing they hadn't turned in their counts yet.

Finding a station that was showing a gubernatorial election for a different state had been interesting. Plus, they were three hours ahead of New Mexico, which meant the coverage hadn't started until ten o'clock at night Eastern time.

It was already midnight in Baltimore, and it looked like it was going to be a long one. Good thing the only person with a regular nine-to-five shift was off the next day.

They had no shortage of entertainment while the talking heads droned on in the background. He could have cut the tension between Erin and Gene with a knife. It was ridiculously thick. Gene had an arm slung along the back of the couch, gazing longingly at the blonde dispatcher. But Erin wasn't looking at him. Instead, she was leaning forward, sitting on the edge of the cushion, her attention on her conversation with Jenna. Roger and Jenna exchanged amused looks throughout the night but didn't say anything. His little Amazon had been right. Something was going on there, but it might be one-sided.

Gene had his sympathy, if it was.

"Oh Jenna, you can move back into the apartment if you want to. The cops finished the investigation."

"Sorry, Erin. Roger asked me to move in with him."

"You mean beyond the election?"

"Yeah." She glanced over at him, and he had to puff his chest a bit at the happiness on her face. "Once it's over, I'm joining his team."

He scoffed. "More like you're going to *be* my team."

"Only until Sam gets here."

Roger raised his bottle and toasted her. "Good point." Sam would be arriving next week, taking over one of his guest rooms for a trial run. Sam's frustration with the FBI had come to a head, and he'd nearly tendered his resignation. Roger had a potential client that had been bugging him about hiring his company for cyber security, which would be Sam's department if everything worked out. Most likely, it would, and Sam would move to Baltimore permanently.

Erin blinked, looking back and forth between them. "Aren't you worried you'll get sick of each other? Living and working with your significant other?"

"Listen, Erin. I'm no spring chicken. I want to soak up as much time with Jenna as possible. Plus, we won't always be on the job together. The point is to be able to accept multiple jobs when possible."

"Gotcha." Erin shook her head and muttered, "Still think you're nuts," under her breath. Roger ignored it. Jenna just shrugged and gave her friend a sheepish grin.

"That's your dad?" Gene asked as he pointed at the screen. Roger watched as Jenna slumped into her seat.

"Yeah. And look, there's my mother."

The news anchors doing political commentary were gone, and the screen had switched to a stage somewhere. An elder statesman in a blue suit and red tie had come to a podium, accompanied by a woman in a mint green skirt suit like his mother used to wear to Easter service. Her light red curls reminded him a bit of Jenna's natural hair color. He'd begged her not to dye it again when she moaned about her roots growing out. The red would suit her more once it came in. And he hated the thought of his Amazon hiding herself anymore.

Governor O'Malley boasted about his platform, and what his win meant for the people of New Mexico. Most of his bloviating went in one ear and out the other, since Roger wasn't familiar with New Mexico politics. But at least now he could openly date Jenna without it being considered a conflict.

"Aren't you happy he won?" Erin asked, taking a swig of her beer and looking at a pouting Jenna.

"Not really. I was rooting for the competition."

Erin's eyes about popped out of her head. "Why? He's your dad."

"And he's kind of an asshole." Jenna sat up and chugged the rest of her beer. "I'm going to get another one. Anyone else?"

Erin and Gene shook their heads. Jenna disappeared into the kitchen. Roger fought the urge to go after her.

"Well, I guess that's that." Erin put her bottle back on the coffee table. "Thanks for having us over."

"Anytime."

Jenna returned as their friends were putting on their coats. "Leaving already?"

"I've been awake since six. I really need to get to bed."

"Aw, okay." The women hugged, and the men shook hands.

Erin still hadn't replaced her car. The insurance company had dragged their feet from what Jenna had shared with him, and Erin wouldn't accept her money, even though Jenna felt responsible. He wondered how Erin planned to get around without a vehicle since she was moving back into her apartment.

Wells opened the door for Erin, desire plain on his face. Maybe there was an answer there. But it wasn't any of Roger's business.

Once their guests were safely in Gene's car and on the road, Roger closed and locked the door. He wrapped his arms around Jenna and leaned back against the wall.

"You okay?"

"I guess." Her eyelids drooped. It could have been because of the beer she'd drank or the fact it was nearly three in the morning.

"You want to talk about it?"

She shrugged. "I guess I just wanted to see him lose for once. My whole life I've never been enough. Maybe it's shitty of me, but it would have been nice for him to see how it feels."

He pulled her close and pressed his lips to the top of her head. "Why don't we go back to ignoring him? He doesn't have any reason to contact me or you. And if any investigators start sniffing around, my security system will catch them."

"It's a thought. A very tempting one." She pushed off from his chest and covered her mouth with a yawn. "I want a shower."

"Do you want company?" He winked.

"Not tonight. I'm too tired."

He gave her a peck on the lips, then patted her curvy ass. "Go ahead then. I'll be right behind you."

Roger double checked that the windows were all closed, the recycling in the bin, and the bowl from the popcorn was sitting in the sink, ready to get washed when they woke up. His final payment from the governor had come through earlier that day, along with the reimbursement for expenses he'd submitted. He turned out the inside lights, leaving his outside lights on for security, and set the alarm.

The bodyguard job was over. And the best part of it for him was that he got to keep Jenna at the end of it.

Hearing the shower turn on, Roger took the stairs two at a time to get to his — no, their — bedroom. Listening to her hum while he stripped his clothes off, Roger smiled like a fool. Jenna's clothes hung in half of his closet. Her former thief tools had their own shelf. And her girly shit was all over the counter in his bathroom.

And as he slid into the bathroom to take his turn, he knew he wouldn't have it any other way.

Epilogue

THE ELECTION WAS OVER, and Jenna and Roger were able to focus on other things. Like family, dying her hair back to red, and getting his baby sister engaged.

"Roger hasn't run any kind of campaign in years. This is going to be fun," an unsuspecting Nadia told Jenna as they tightened each other's bracers. Then Nadia turned to her friends, who'd come along for the "shake and bake" LARP event Roger had arranged in his backyard. Between him and Erin, they were all outfitted with weapons and a few pieces of armor.

Of the players, only Roger, Caleb, and Jon knew the true purpose. They'd clued Jenna in as well. Finn was already in the Middle East somewhere, but Sam had helped set up video cameras to record the event and send it to him later. Caleb didn't want to leave anyone out. Sam refused to play with them, so he was inside the house with Judy and Irving, watching everything on his screens.

A tall Black woman, one of Nadia's friends, shook her head. "This is your idea of fun?"

"Come on, Jade. It's not that different from cosplay." A short, curvy blonde with pink tips in her hair said.

"Except most cosplayers aren't trying to hit you with their weapons."

The other blonde, a skinny girl with her hair in twin buns, nodded. "True, those things take ages to build."

"Everyone ready?" Jenna asked the group. When they nodded, she gave Roger the wave they'd worked out to let him know the game could begin. He walked around to the front of his house to collect Jon and get started.

Dressed in full garb, they came running around the opposite side of the house. "Asteria!"

Nadia's head snapped to look at him. "Yes, General?"

Right, that was Nadia's in-game name.

"Have you seen Corvon? He never came back from patrol last night."

"No, I haven't."

"We can't find him anywhere."

Jon spoke up this time. "Rumor has it these woods are teeming with orcs. Do you think he ran afoul of them?"

Rustling from the bushes behind them made all the players turn and look. A green-tinted face peeked between branches, then pulled back.

"Holy shit," Nadia breathed. She looked back at Roger. "Should we follow it?"

He nodded and motioned for his sister to lead. "Let's go."

The party spread out, heading off to the left, where the orc had vanished. Jenna scouted ahead, confirmed they were where they were supposed to be, then returned when Regen gave her a nod.

She sidled up next to her boyfriend. "General, I count seven orcs."

He made a show of rubbing his chin in thought. "A hunting party. That makes sense."

"And you think they have Corvon?" Nadia actually looked worried. She must really get into her character.

Jon shrugged. "I can't imagine why else he wouldn't return from patrol."

And then, just like they'd planned it, came Caleb's cry. "Mercy!"

"Cal-Corvon!" Nadia gasped. Holy shit, she'd nearly broke character. Jenna smirked at Roger over Nadia's head.

For a moment, Roger grinned like an idiot back at her, then twisted his face into a war cry. Jon and the ladies all followed suit as he led their charge into the orc encampment.

Except Nadia did something they didn't expect. Roger explained when they made their plans that his sister normally started in the back of a battle with her bow, and then moved to her melee weapon when she ran out of arrows. This time? She ignored her bow completely and charged right into the center of the chaos! The orcs had instructions not to impede her too much, but the blond, muscular one Roger had referred to as Cillian apparently didn't care. He rose in front of her and their swords smacked together. Nadia threw herself at him, putting everything she had into her sword fight.

Beyond Cillian, they had tied Caleb to a tree at the edge of the clearing, red paint on his garb to look like torture wounds. Regen, the orc Jenna was busy fighting, saw the same thing she did.

"Damn it, he went off-script!" They looked at each other over their crossed swords. "Pretend to cut my head off and go help her." Jenna nodded and mimed a chopping motion at the base of Regen's neck, leaving them to fall in a dramatic death scene.

She bolted for Nadia, and Roger must have had the same idea. Together, they attacked Cillian, giving Nadia a chance to breathe.

"Corvon!" Nadia cried as she flung herself at her beloved. "Are you alright?"

"Asteria, my love..." he hacked a very believable cough. "I never thought I'd see you again."

Shit, he was a good actor. Nadia was almost in tears as she kissed him and pulled the ropes away as a cheer went up from the Melberth team.

Caleb gave Nadia a moment to bask in the victory, and the defeated orcs rose from the ground. Then, holding her hand, he turned to face her and fell to one knee.

She spun to look at him, concern etched on her face. "Corvon?"

Her boyfriend shook his head and reached inside a pouch on his hip, pulling out a ring. "Nadia, you have rescued me in so many ways. You rescued my dad from the thief he hired. You helped me heal from my mother's abandonment. You showed me I deserve love and rescued me from a boring life. You're strong, stubborn —"

"Hear, hear!" cried Roger, with the biggest grin on his face. His outburst drew laughs from the audience.

Nadia stuck her tongue out at him, then turned back to Caleb, who was shaking his head.

"—and I wouldn't change a single thing. Even when we're arguing, you make me want to be a better man. And there's no one else I'd rather fight through life with."

Nadia's friends had gathered in a group hug, and Jenna could hear their sniffling from where she stood. She blinked hard at the wetness gathering in her eyes.

"Nadia Lynn Hunt, will you marry me?"

Nadia's tearful voice carried through the clearing. "Caleb Gray, I am covered in dirt and sweat, my bun is coming undone, and you're asking me... to *marry* you?" He bit his lip and nodded, still kneeling in the grass. "My answer... is YES!"

She screamed the last word, and the whole clearing applauded and cheered. Caleb wore the biggest grin as he slipped the ring on her finger, then stood, and bent her back in a deep kiss. When he pulled her upright, her four friends descended on them in a tearful group hug.

FRANKIE LOOKED DOWN AT the address she'd written down on paper, old-school style. Then she squinted at the street sign. This was their street, alright. She put her boot back up on the foot peg of her motorcycle and turned slowly down the gravel driveway.

Finally, *finally* she could see the house that satellite imaging hadn't been able to get close to. Clearly the man valued his privacy. Frankie respected that. But he'd issued the invitation for her to visit. It had taken her longer than she'd wanted, but she finally had the information she needed and erased herself from the syndicate.

Her findings had horrified her, and she knew Foxy would want to know about them. If Fox was the kind of woman Frankie thought she was, then she'd want to take the syndicate down, too.

This wasn't just a friends' catching up trip. She'd come here to find allies in her upcoming war.

Vehicles lined the front lawn and the gravel in front of the detached three-car garage. The unmistakable scent of meat cooking over a flame tantalized her nostrils. Well, shit. She hadn't expected to be crashing a party as well.

Sauntering around the house, she narrowed her eyes and tilted her head to the side. There on the back lawn was a group of grown men and women fighting each other in medieval armor and weapons. On her second look, the weapons appeared to be made of foam. Looking around, she recognized Roger from the photo on his website for Hunt Security. He manned the grill on the back patio, laughing with a redhead and pointing at the spectacle. Could they know those weirdoes?

They'd never exchanged pictures. She hoped it wouldn't take Jenna long to figure out who she was.

"Hey, foxy lady!" She called out with a grin. The redhead and Roger both turned to look at her.

"Frankie! You're here!" Yup, that was Jenna. She vaulted over the railing and ran to Frankie for a hug. "Perfect timing. We're just about to cook the burgers."

A lovely offer, but Frankie was there on business. "Listen, girlfriend, we gotta have a chat."

Jenna released her, her face sober. "About what?"

"Work," she sighed, looking at the crowd gathered. "But it can wait until after the party."

"Sounds serious."

Frankie just shrugged. "I didn't mean to crash. I should have called ahead."

Jenna waved her off. "There's plenty of food. Come on, I'll introduce you."

The party went well into the evening. Clean-up didn't start until the sun went down, but with all the people crammed around the table, it didn't take long. Then everyone was saying their goodbyes. Frankie hung back, trying to ignore the guilt creeping up at crashing the party. But then she brought up the faces of the women she'd seen on the camera and reminded herself her mission was more important than her pride.

After all was said and done, the only people who remained at the house were Roger, Jenna, Frankie, and

Roger's friend, Sam. Apparently he was on vacation and staying in the house. As the guys drank beer and shot the shit, Frankie pulled Jenna aside and into the kitchen.

"You remember how I was going to investigate our... former employer?"

She nodded.

"Well, I found out what those gems were funding."

Jenna's brow furrowed. "What?"

Frankie leaned in, not wanting the guys to overhear them. "Trafficking."

Wide blue eyes met hers when she pulled back. "Do you have proof?"

She nodded. "I can't just drop it off with the authorities, though. They have people in their pocket and it's going to take time to figure out who'd be safe."

Jenna's face had gone ghost white. It looked like the realization had taken a moment to fully hit her. "Oh, my God... sex trafficking?"

Frankie nodded slowly. "That's why I had to leave. I couldn't be a part of it anymore." A shudder ran down her back, and she had to force the images she'd seen away to ensure her delicious dinner didn't make a reappearance.

Jenna clutched her stomach like she might throw up. "What do we do?"

Frankie crossed her arms over her ample chest. "I'm going to end it. Are you with me?"

"Hell yes." Jenna reached out, and they clasped hands.

"Hell yes to what?" Roger asked as he and his friend wandered into the kitchen.

Frankie eyed the men. Jenna had vouched for Roger being a good guy, and *he* knew all about their past. Sam, on the other hand, was a stranger, and she didn't know how much he knew.

Jenna turned to her man. If she trusted Sam enough for him to be in the room, Frankie would trust her judgment. She'd second guessed Jenna once before and it had backfired pretty spectacularly.

"Frankie says the syndicate is running a human trafficking ring. She wants me to help end it."

The men's eyes nearly popped out of their skulls. "Count me in." Roger extended a hand the size of a dinner plate at her, and Frankie nearly squeaked. As a short, plus-sized girl, she got intimidated by big men. That was why she was more comfortable behind the keyboard. But Roger's handshake was firm yet gentle, demonstrating a level of respect she wasn't sure she deserved.

"I'm in, too." Sam drew her attention his way. She'd been trying to avoid looking at that tall drink of milk all day. His blonde curls looked soft as hell, and he had serious blue eyes behind those wire frames.

"And what do you do?" That came out wrong. She didn't mean to sound like a bitch. "I mean, I know what he does," she gestured to Roger. "But what about you?"

She swore his eyes twinkled. "FBI, Cyber Crimes division. I'm visiting from Colorado."

Oh, good goddamn. Of course, she had to be attracted to a Fed.

Hang on a minute. Jenna had said Roger had a contact at the FBI when she threatened to turn states' evidence. Could this be the guy that caught her trail?

Frankie wondered if she'd gone from the frying pan right into the flame, but those women deserved all the help she could give them.

Also By Jasmine

For a current list of my available titles, scan the QR code below:

About the Author

I inherited my love of reading from my parents. As the daughter of two teachers, one of whom is also a librarian, I was the kid who walked out of the library with the maximum number of books each week, then walked back in the following week having read every single one. This would go on all summer long. When I could put pencil to paper, I started writing my own (terrible) kid's stories. Around age eight, I told my mom I wanted to be an author when I grew up, but she talked me out of it. She wanted me to have a stable career because of my poor health.

While I learned to manage my chronic condition through childhood, I also kept writing as a creative outlet. But when I grew up and turned my focus to my career, writing went by the wayside. The stories would not come again until quarantine in 2020 when trauma from the year before poured out of me in a cathartic story now known as *Roar for Me*. The decision to self-publish was an easy one. I consider each book its own work of art and I want to control not only what I write, but all the packaging, as well.

I write books I want to read. This means intelligent characters, happy-ever-afters, and no cheating. Adult contemporary romances with plenty of steam appeal to me the most. Music and pop culture are my biggest sources of inspiration. And I love to flip the script and surprise readers by putting a twist on their expectations.

Everyone deserves their own love story. I've always believed that. I want to develop a wide range of characters so everyone can relate to someone in one of my books. I especially love challenging gender expectations. And I hope my books will be an escape for readers, not just entertainment. When I'm not writing, I'm working in healthcare in my native Pittsburgh. Or you might find me crafting, baking sweet treats, or playing *Mario Kart* with my own nerdy love.

Notes From Jasmine

Thank you for reading Roger and Jenna's story! I hope you enjoyed my first foray into romantic suspense. And I hope for the readers who loved Nadia's brothers in The Geek Girl Squad, that you enjoy how their stories play out in the books to come.

I'd like to thank Maria Secoy, my coach and critique partner, for her wisdom and assistance. To my beta team, your comments give me life! Jenn, my editor, who is as varied as me in her interests, thanks for joining me on this genre pivot! Somehow no matter what direction I turn you're always there cheering me on and I am so grateful. Sarah Kil, for making me stop scrolling in her Facebook group and exclaim "Oh my God, that's Roger!" during her premade sale. I'm so excited to keep working with you on these covers.

As always, thanks for the YouTube videos, Dale L. Roberts, Jenna Moreci, Sasha Black, and Abbie Emmons.

XOXO,

Jasmine